Wandering Through Time

Wandering Through Time

The Collected Short Fiction (So Far)

by Ian Randal Strock

FANTASTIC
BOOKS

Fantastic Books
1380 East 17 Street, Suite 2233
Brooklyn, New York 11230
www.FantasticBooks.biz

ISBN: 978-1-5154-5822-7

First Edition

For Mom, Dad, and Laurie: for everything.

Contents

It's not "the lady or the tiger?", it's "which tiger?"

(first published in
Analog Science Fiction and Fact, April 2014)

I have a long history with Analog. *I was the editorial assistant, and then the assistant editor, and then the associate editor, from 1989 to 1995. My first professional story appeared in the September 1992 issue of the magazine ("Fermat's Legacy," later in this volume), and since then, I've had more stories in the magazine, letters, a science article, even a guest editorial, but this story, in the April 2014 issue, marked the first appearance of my name on the cover of the magazine.*

"You look depressed. Want to talk about it?"

Archetypal bartender, but there's a reason for the archetype. "Not really. But I have a feeling I'm going to anyway."

"So talk. It may help, and it certainly won't hurt."

Pretty good archetypal bartender.

"I'm an entrepreneur, a typical one. I can feel success drawing me forward. I know there's going to be success in here somewhere… or at least, I really hope there's going to be success. But this one is just as big a failure as the previous four. And after I sober up tomorrow morning, I'm going to have to let my staff go and tell my investors that this business, too, is just not meant to be. How many times can one man do that, and still be able to look at himself in the mirror in the morning?"

Long silence; the bartender's losing points. "Oh, that wasn't rhetorical? Most folks in here, they ask questions, but they treat me like a psychiatrist, not really wanting input."

"I'm not most folks. Most folks aren't serial failures at business."

"You'd be surprised. But no, most of them don't launch their own companies in order to fail. Is that what you're trying to do? Fail? Do you have a certain number of failures in mind, before you find that success?"

"What kind of jerk would I have to be to plan to fail…" Oh, I get it. He picked up on that "typical entrepreneur" bit. "You think I'm aiming for the same number of failures as the average?"

"How could I possibly think that? I've just met you. But I have seen a lot of people sitting where you are, crying over failures. And in many cases, they're self-inflicted."

"Now you're saying I sabotaged my own businesses."

"And now you're looking to blame someone else for what was probably just bad market conditions."

Bartender's stock heads back up. "You've got a point. Got a suggestion to go with it?"

"If I could give you the kind of suggestion you're really looking for, I wouldn't be standing behind a bar."

"I don't know. There are times when what you do has appeal. Less responsibility, some security, you immediately know if you're doing a good job or not."

"We're not talking about me right now. Back to you: what keeps you going? Why do you get out of bed in the morning? Why do you go to work? Why did you start—five, was it?—businesses, rather than chucking it all and sitting in the park talking to squirrels?"

"Faith in myself, I guess. The inner knowledge that I'm going to succeed."

"Knowledge?"

"If it were just a hope, I probably would have given up. There's some spark in me that tells me I'm going to succeed. I'm going to start a business that will grow, flourish, make people's lives better, and not coincidentally, make me wealthy and famous."

"Now you're starting to sound a little more 'regular guy' to me. That 'wealth and fame' part, that's a bigger driver than you usually admit out loud, isn't it?"

"Well, now that you mention it, yes, it is. But is there anything wrong with that?"

"Nothing wrong with wanting to be famous. Tending bar these many years, it seems to me what's wrong is not admitting your own desires to yourself."

"All right, I admit it: I want to be rich and famous. And I think the way to do it is to start a business that everyone wants to patronize, that people will admire."

"Fair enough. Now, what if I could tell you, with absolute certainty, that you're going to die in two years. Would you do something different? Would you keep doing what you're doing? That's something I ask myself every couple of years. That question is why I left sales, and day trading, and truck driving. And it's why I've been standing behind this bar for a decade, serving drinks, talking with people, providing for my family."

"That's a difficult question for an entrepreneur. The average start-up takes four years before we can tell if it's a success or a failure. If every entrepreneur had to work with a two-year horizon, no businesses could be started."

"I wasn't asking that. If the death of one person dooms a company, doesn't that say the company isn't strong enough to survive very long anyway?"

"That's a point."

"That's what makes this a difficult question, and therefore, an important one. How many times did you, as a boss, deal with easy questions, and how often did you hire someone to handle them, so you could focus on the difficult ones?"

"You're right. The difficult questions are the important ones."

"So, back to my difficult question: you've got two years to live. Do you keep doing what you're doing? Or do you go off and do something else?"

"Two years, huh?"

"Two years. It's long enough that the proper answer can't be to drop everything and party, but not so long that you can ignore it."

"I'm going to have to think on that. But I came in here to not think for this evening."

"No, you didn't."

"Contradicting me? That's not very bartenderish."

"Sure it is. If you wanted to turn off your brain for the evening, you would have gone to the movies. But you came in here, where there's nothing to occupy your mind, because you wanted to think about things. I'm just helping you focus those thoughts."

"All right. Give me another drink, and let me think."

He places a full glass in front of me. "Group down the end needs another round. I'll be back."

I hold my glass, not drinking, staring at the wonderful shapes and colors of the bottles behind the bar, just letting my vision drift until I'm not seeing much of anything.

"I couldn't help overhearing," says a quiet voice beside me.

I blink back into the here-now, and turn to look at… the most non-descript person I've ever seen. Well, that's not fair. He does look somewhat familiar, though I'm sure I can't place him. But there's something about him that just blends into the crowd, as if he's trying to not be noticed.

"Sorry, I was zoning."

"I said, 'I couldn't help overhearing you'," he repeat-continues. "I understand your frustration. You feel like you're not getting anywhere, perhaps even backsliding, and there's no way to dig out from under it all, to get to the top of the heap."

"Something like that," I say.

"That bartender asked a good question, though: what if you had only a short time to live?"

"That's what I was mulling over when you sat down."

"So try talking it out. Short time to live, coming off a failed business—"

I glare at him, but he waves it away.

"You said so yourself. So what do you do now? Start the next, knowing you might not live to see it mature? Or get out of the entrepreneurship thing all together. Put on a suit and tie, print up a resume, and fall into an office job. You'd be able to draw a salary, do what you wanted on the weekends, feel the security of income and benefits."

"Yes, but the appeal of that…"

"Is limited. I know. Sitting at a desk, following someone else's nine-to-five, being just one among many, undistinguished, gray—"

"You do understand." My brain clicks back into alert-mode.

"And you know that would be kinder to your family, to your friends who worry about your future."

"Yes, exactly. My security would ease their minds. But—wait a minute. Do I know you?"

"No. At least, not yet. But, I'm someone who can guarantee your security."

"What, are you offering me a desk job?"

"No. I don't have one to offer. I have something better… and, potentially, worse."

"Now you're talking in riddles, friend."

"That bartender's hypothetical was closer to reality than he knew. I'm from the future… grandfather."

I look more closely. I stare at him, hard. Yeah, maybe, kind of, maybe around the eyes, a little, he starts to look sort of familiar. No. No way. My grandson? "Grandfather? Is that a joke? I don't even have kids."

"Yet." He stares back at me. "My grandmother is about six weeks pregnant with your son, right now."

"We broke up a month ago."

"I know. That's why my father never gets the chance to meet you."

"All right. You've piqued my interest."

"First, a philosophical question, grandfather. What would you risk for success?"

"Nothing philosophical about it," I grump. "I've already done it, four, no, five times now. I risked just about everything. I've been sleeping on friends' couches when I wasn't living with my parents, working twenty-six hour days, as long as possible, to drive each company's success. And I've been strangling my own metaphorical children—those selfsame companies—when I realized it was time to let them go. I think my life has pretty much answered the question 'What would I risk for success?'."

"No, I'm talking bigger stakes."

I'm starting to think he really could be related to me. "Like what?"

"I came back to offer you comfort, love, happiness, a life of ease. You've earned it, grandfather. Five start-up and shut-down businesses. I know you've worried that it'll kill you before you find that success you've been trying for."

"So what are you offering?"

"Let me take you to the future with me. I have a very nice home and a happy life. You'd have security, comfort, no worries. You would be welcome, your great-grandchildren would love to meet you, and I'd like the chance to get to know you. Our medical knowledge would keep you healthy and comfortable for a long time to come."

"And what is the price of this wonderful boon you're offering me?" I can see in his eyes that he knows more.

"I overheard most of your conversation with the bartender."

"You mean about my need for fame, public adulation, some kind of external recognition."

"I had a hunch about that, even before I came here. And that's what you'd be giving up. I can keep you healthy and comfortable, and even, I think, happy, to a degree. But as an anachronism in my time, you wouldn't have any chance at achieving the kind of fame you've been craving."

"Then why are you here? What is this, some twisted Faust deal?"

"No, no, nothing like that. I'm just trying to give you all the facts, before I explain why I think it would be a good choice for you."

"You're saying giving up my soul to secure my body is a good choice?"

"I think it would be, grandfather. In the original time line, your sixth attempt was a success. A massive success. Huge growth, international appeal, the company turned into a modern-day empire, and your name was known around the globe."

"Now I'm confused."

"That was your legacy, not your life. You… well, there's no good way to say this. You died late in the start-up phase."

"How late?"

"You launched the company, and started growing it, when you died suddenly, about two years after the start, and less than a month before the first big angel investor pumped in the money that drove, well, everything else. It's all your idea, and fully acknowledged. The company was renamed for you, and you found that fame beyond your wildest dreams. But you weren't around to enjoy it."

I stare at him, my mind a whirl.

"It did, however, provide a very comfortable life for my father, as it does for me and my children. But I never got to meet you. And my father wasn't told of his relationship to you until he was a teenager."

"My sixth start-up, you say? My next corporate attempt?"

"Yes."

"So that means soon?"

"Yes."

"So you're here—"

"You should have the long life you're destined for. You should enjoy your family and a life of ease, after all these years of hardship and toil and loneliness."

I hug my grandson, this man who is, I realize, years older than I am.

I put my still-untouched second drink on the bar, and the bartender comes back.

"That's a lot of thought, if you haven't yet started this drink."

"I realized I don't need a drink. I need to get a good night's sleep, because tomorrow morning I have to shut down my fifth business, and get started on my sixth."

Shall Not Perish from the Earth
(first published in the anthology
Altered States of the Union)

This story was my first written specifically for an anthology. Glenn Hauman, the editor, asked me to write a story for his anthology of alternate history stories, focusing on what things would be like if the United States had evolved—politically—differently than it has (outside of science fiction, because I'm the author of three books on presidential history). I immediately thought of Abraham Lincoln, the Civil War, and the Great Compromise of 1787. As a presidential historian, one might assume I knew everything there was to know about Lincoln. But I'm a bit of a contrarian; I focus far more on lesser-knowns, the uncommons, the oddities. So I had to do quite a bit of research to write this story. Glenn liked it so much, he made it the lead story in the anthology.

From the *Encyclopedia Americana*:
  The founders of the United States of America created a document that allowed disparate states to act together cohesively to form a greater union. Unlike the empires with which the founders were familiar, the Constitution granted the smaller portions a greater degree of control of the central government. To avoid the tyranny of the ruler, they set the capital to roaming about the country, moving from state to state each decade. To give

all the constituent units a say in the government, they created a legislature comprised of two representatives from each state (the Senate). And to maintain a system of checks and balances, a Supreme Court....

In the middle of the 19th Century, the growing divide between the Northern and Southern states over the issue of slavery created increasing factionalism and strain on the union. Presidents Franklin Pierce and James Buchanan attempted appeasement from the capital in Concord, New Hampshire, as a strategy to keep the union together. Southern interests were agitated, but knew that the capital would be moving to Columbia, South Carolina, following the election of 1860....

In 1856, out of the remains of the now-defunct Whig party, the Republicans formed and ran their first candidate for President. John C. Frémont won one-third of the popular vote, and the votes of the eleven Northernmost states. He lost handily to Democrat James Buchanan, while former President Millard Fillmore—this time the standard-bearer for the American party—won the electoral votes of Maryland. It was not an inspiring showing for the Republicans, but it was something to build on.

Abraham Lincoln came to national prominence with his abolitionist speeches during his own failed political campaign: Stephen Douglas defeated him in 1858 in their campaign for a seat in the Senate representing Illinois. But Lincoln impressed enough people that he was invited to New York to give a speech before a powerful group of Republicans at Cooper Union. That speech catapulted him to the forefront of the race for the Republican nomination in the home state of two of his chief rivals: William Seward and Salmon Chase (both of whom would wind up serving in Lincoln's Presidential Cabinet).

In May of 1860, the Republicans nominated Lincoln for President, with Senator Hannibal Hamlin from Maine as his Vice Presidential running mate.

The Democrats, meanwhile, were suffering from party factionalism to mimic that of the country. The Northern branch of the party nominated Lincoln's old nemesis and fellow Illinoisan, Stephen Douglas, for President. The Southerners, however, threw their support behind Vice President John C. Breckinridge.

The stage was set for a landmark election. The Republicans, having formed as the anti-slavery party, were nearly by definition the anti-Southern party. Curiously, Lincoln himself took almost no part in the election of 1860. Instead, he stayed home and monitored the proceedings, while his party faithful advertised, wrote, campaigned, and spoke, spreading the word.

If nothing else, the results showed that the United States of America was a starkly divided nation. Lincoln took all the Northern states, Breckinridge the Southern. Douglas—who was himself a fence-sitter on the issue of slavery, not favoring it but not urging its abolition—won only the state of Missouri, itself a fence-sitter, being Northern but permitting slavery.

When the results were made known, Southerners seethed their disapproval. Slavery was an institution, a way of life; and its abolition, they assumed, would bring financial ruin and Northern domination to their home states.

Radical elements in the South urged dissolution of the union, breaking away from the North before Lincoln could be inaugurated and set his plans in motion. But cooler heads prevailed. The national capital, after all, would be spending the next decade in Columbia, South Carolina, seat of the South. With the capital in their pocket, Lincoln's promises could be thwarted, he could be made to see reason, or, as a last resort...

Following his election, Lincoln planned a whistle-stop train tour to take him east from his home in Illinois, through several Northern states, and then South to inaugurate the decade in Columbia and begin his own term as President. He chose to bypass the New England states. The capital was at that time leaving Concord, New Hampshire, but New England was out of Lincoln's way, and Vice President-elect Hannibal Hamlin—a native of Maine—was delegated to stand-in for Lincoln at the farewell ceremonies.

Early in February, as Lincoln was beginning his journey, security officer Allan Pinkerton warned him of an assassination plot, and urged him to bypass Baltimore and travel the rest of the way to Columbia in haste and in secret.

Lincoln's long-time friend, Ward Hill Lamon, who also took on the self-appointed role of Lincoln's bodyguard, dismissed Pinkerton's warning as fantasy. He feared that sneaking into the new capital would make Lincoln look weak at a time when he needed to show strength.

In the end, Lincoln chose caution. He hurried through Baltimore late at night, avoiding the crowds and the potential danger, and driving a wedge between Lamon and Pinkerton. No one knew of the deception until Mary Lincoln and their children arrived on the regularly scheduled train the following afternoon. They were greeted by crowds, but those crowds—including any lurking assassins—were disappointed at missing the President-elect.

Lincoln resumed his public voyage south of Baltimore, and arrived safely in Columbia at the end of February. He was greeted with the honors Presidents-elect had come to expect since George Washington's arrival in New York City. The new national capital building—which was scheduled to become the new capital of South Carolina in 1870, following the departure of the federal government to a Northern capital—was ready, and retiring President James Buchanan greeted Lincoln as a friend. Buchanan had arrived two days earlier, on a special train from Concord, accompanied by incoming Vice President Hannibal Hamlin.

At the time, little notice was paid to the missing Senators, though they would loom large in history. Specifically, seven newly elected Senators from Northern states who had not yet arrived in Columbia. The 61 Senators who were present attended Abraham Lincoln's inauguration and inaugural speech. Later that afternoon, the Senators were sworn in by the new Vice President. The absence of the seven was noted in the minutes of the special session of Congress. Senator Nesmith, of Oregon, was assumed to have been delayed in his long journey. Some surprise was expressed at the absence of Senators

Lane and Pomeroy—new state Kansas's first members in the legislative body. The other four, however, were merely assumed to be absent.

President Abraham Lincoln had come to office on the Republican platform of ending slavery, and after nominating his Cabinet, he set about writing legislation to bring about the abolition his party sought.

That was when he realized the import of those missing Senators. Even though his fellow Illinoisan Lyman Trumbull was available to introduce his legislation, and Vice President Hamlin was fulfilling his role of presiding over the body's deliberations, those seven vacant seats meant the Southerners had an effective majority in the Senate, and could dictate its actions, regardless of the President's desires.

Lincoln via Trumbull introduced several pieces of legislation—attempts to curtail or end slavery—during the three weeks the Senate was in town. All of them were voted down with a minimum of fuss.

Following long-standing tradition, the Senate adjourned at the end of March, and the Senators scattered.

There was an outbreak of smallpox in Columbia in December of 1860, and at that time, there was discussion of shifting the capital to Charleston for health reasons, but at such a late date, a move was deemed impossible. Instead, authorities in Columbia downplayed the extent of the smallpox outbreak, and Lincoln was never even advised of it.

Thus, after battling the Senate for three long weeks, Lincoln viewed the adjournment—without legislative action—with a certain degree of relief. He retired to his bed for nearly a month, and though the word was that he was exhausted, modern evidence suggests he was in fact suffering from a mild case of smallpox. It was never formally diagnosed, and the few resultant scars were most probably hidden by Lincoln's life-long poor complexion. And while smallpox does not become chronic, it is assumed that Lincoln's case damaged his respiratory system, leaving him more susceptible to later ailments.

After recovering from the depression of his first three wholly ineffective weeks dealing with the Senate (and possibly from smallpox), Lincoln spent the month of April setting up his government, receiving foreign ambassadors, touring the new capital city, and talking with the few reporters who'd bothered to stay in town. But he knew he wasn't accomplishing very much, and making no inroads toward his goal of abolishing slavery.

He tried to integrate himself with the local culture, but found himself repeatedly rebuffed as an outsider: respected as President, but viewed with suspicion and trepidation as a Northerner, especially one who loudly and publicly agitated for abolition.

He was a stranger in a strange land; an oddity on display, but little respected.

The problem with truly effective conspiracies is that they are secret. Even today, we may never know the full extent of the machinations against Lincoln, especially in the Spring of 1861. It is known that Senator Jefferson Davis—who had been Secretary of War during Franklin Pierce's administration, and who was a Southerner, from

Mississippi—was involved, however reluctantly. In his personal writings, Davis expressed his misgivings of what was to come. But he viewed himself as a patriot: loyal to his native Mississippi. And Mississippi, as part of the South, was a slave state and opposed to Northern domination, so Davis did all he could to support the cause.

Also known was William Henry Gist—formerly the governor of South Carolina, he had refused to seek another term, rather than play the genial host to the federal government headed by Lincoln—who was definitely one of the underground leaders.

Beyond Davis and Gist, however, the cabal is still nameless and faceless. It surely included the household staff assigned to the President, as well as most of the city government who were hosting.

What is known of the cabal is its effectiveness. In an era not far removed from George Washington's invisible ink and letter-transposition codes, they managed to intercept nearly all communications to and from the office of the President.

Davis must have been involved in the near-continuous rewriting work that kept Lincoln supplied with the correct volume of cables, letters, and wires, while modifying their content and moving to isolate Lincoln…

A scrap of paper in Lincoln's hand, assumed to be a fragment of a now-lost diary:

What's happened to me? I came to Columbia full of excitement. We were going to change the world, fulfill the promise of the Declaration. We've been here two months, accomplished

*nothing, and I seem to have lost all the hopes I
had after the election.*

*Mary recommends that I "enjoy being the
President for a while, rather than trying to force
the issue."*

*"Enjoy" seems horribly inappropriate, when
so many live in bondage, but she keeps pushing
me to "Get out. Travel around. Maybe take a trip
home, feel some Northern adulation."*

In May, before the cabal had solidified its control
over Lincoln, he tried to call the Senate into special
session. He'd spent two months recovering from
smallpox and fuming over his ineffectiveness, and
finally, he had had enough. The cabal was unable to stop
the call from going out, but they were able to piggyback
onto it a notice to Southern Senators, and those thirty
Southerners rejected the call (all but Mississippi's
Jefferson Davis, who had remained in Columbia as part
of the cabal, to keep up his campaign of Presidential
miscommunication and misdirection). And thus, once
again, the seven missing Senators changed the course of
events. The thirty Southerners were a minority of the
full-strength Senate, but the seven—who had not arrived
before the Senate adjourned in March—were not
counted in the Senate's membership, and would not be
until the Senate, in session, swore them in and accepted
them as members.

The Senate did not meet in the summer of 1861.

Lincoln's first summer as President saw a remarkable
change in his personality. The formerly gregarious,

outgoing lawyer became taciturn, almost non-communicative. Indeed, other than appearances at Independence Day celebrations, Lincoln was not seen in public until late October. And this long absence did not go unnoticed by the cabal.

The Senate finally returned in December, and the formerly missing Senators were present, each arriving with a harrowing tale of danger or threats that had kept him from entering the South. Though it was a federal crime to interfere with a Senator's attendance to a duly called session, none of the seven could identify their attackers. And once again, the pervasive Southern sentiment surrounding the government was sufficient to quash further investigations. "They are here now: we should look to the future, not the past," became a mantra, headlining editorials, and titling a popular song.

In the end, the Senate's investigation was cursory, inconclusive, and forgotten.

With a full Senate—nine months after Lincoln's inauguration—the President finally had hopes of pushing through his legislative agenda.

Those hopes were quickly dashed.

Lincoln's first proposal for a Constitutional amendment outlawing slavery died quietly in committee. As did his less sweeping proposals to limit its expansion. Meanwhile, competing proposals reaffirming states' rights clogged up the legislative agenda.

Despite his role as President of the Senate, Hannibal Hamlin knew there was almost nothing he could do, and there were times during the session of 1861–62 that he discussed with Lincoln the possibility of resigning.

* * *

From *The Autobiography of Hannibal Hamlin*:

"John Adams called it 'the most insignificant office that ever the invention of man contrived.' And as this session dragged on, I knew more and more what he meant. But beyond the uselessness of the Vice Presidency, I felt even more ineffective as President of the Senate. President Lincoln, however, convinced me to stay. 'We are an embassy of Northern rationality in this cesspool of slave-owners,' he told me in a private moment. 'If you were to leave, what support would I have? It would be ceding the whole government, the entirety of the United States of America, to the scourge of slavery.' And so I promised to soldier on with him. Indeed, seeing how passionate he was—how frustrated, but still so passionate—I returned to the Senate with renewed vigor, and a renewed determination to bring about the true freedom for which we both fought."

Hamlin's new-found strength to push back against the Southern obstructionists was met with threats. Hamlin never did reveal who he spoke with, but soon he was reporting back to Lincoln of concrete threats of secession.

Lincoln, fearing the possibility of presiding over a government in enemy territory, told Hamlin to back down, and the session of December 1862, opened with amity amongst the Senators. No real business was accomplished, but neither did seething distrust break out into open rebellion.

* * *

In February of 1862, 11-year-old Willie Lincoln—the second of the President's three surviving children—contracted a severe case of typhoid, and died.

This loss affected Lincoln almost as much as Mary. The illness, it is also assumed, exasperated Lincoln's lingering respiratory problems from his bout of smallpox.

Whether it was only mourning, or mourning combined with his own sickness, Lincoln was not seen for several weeks, as he remained cloistered with Mary in their apartment.

Wrangling the government nearly single-handedly was a much larger job than Vice President Hamlin expected at that point, and the resultant overwhelm forced him to focus on the day-to-day operations of the government at the expense of the Republicans' planned legislative package. The Southern Senators took advantage of this feebleness, and nothing further happened during that session.

When the Senate adjourned in 1862—having accomplished nothing other than thwarting the President's legislative agenda at every turn—Lincoln joined the exodus, returning home for the first time since his departure a year and a half earlier. His immediate plans were to mourn the loss of Willie and to recuperate.

He had planned several whistle stops on his journey home, but the first few, in the Carolinas and Virginia, proved so disappointing that he told his staff to cancel the rest, and just run on through. Mary, however, urged him to continue with the original plans, if only to show that he was still the President and still in charge.

When the train reached Pennsylvania, the crowds that greeted him reminded Lincoln that he truly was President of a divided country. Indeed, the adulation and support he received at every stop north of the Mason-Dixon Line was like a revivifying tonic, and those traveling with him remarked on his changed appearance. He stood straighter, spoke with a stronger voice, and seemed to grow younger as the journey continued.

By the time the Presidential train reached Illinois, Lincoln seemed to be on the campaign trail, running hard, rather than simply greeting well-wishers. He accepted their condolences for the loss of Willie, but the burden of that loss seemed to have lifted along the railway.

At home, Lincoln rested, recovered from the strains of the office, and remembered what he was struggling for.

One notable event during the President's sojourn in Illinois was his meeting with Ulysses Grant. The former soldier was living in Galena, struggling through a series of failed business ventures. Upon Lincoln's election, Grant had sensed impending military action, and managed to get himself appointed a colonel to train up volunteers. And when Lincoln was home in 1862, they met. Grant left the meeting with a Presidential promotion to brigadier general, and a Presidential command to expeditiously increase the number of trained soldiers across the North.

In letters he exchanged with Hamlin over the summer, it was clear that the Vice President's experiences were similar to Lincoln's: the journey home was medicine for his soul. Lincoln asked Hamlin to join him in Illinois for the trip back to Columbia in November.

Optimists seeing the President and Vice President on their return to the seat of government saw a triumphal procession, supporting their champion on the way to battle. But pessimists feared it was a valedictory journey, and that they would not see Lincoln alive again.

The timbre of the crowds changed immediately as the train entered the South, but Lincoln carried the memory of his months at home with him, and used it as a cloak to fend off the condemnation of those few Southerners who turned out to see him.

By the time the Senate convened in December, 1862, the energized Lincoln and Hamlin had planned out a full legislative agenda: limiting slavery, strengthening the federal government, and funding the trans-continental railroad. They knew they faced an uphill battle: the recent elections promised to make the Senate an even-more polarized body, if that was possible. But those ten seat changes would not happen until March. There was still time, or so they thought.

The lame-duck session, however, proved even more skittish. Senators were completely unwilling to debate any issue more contentious than what to have for dinner. Legislation died in committee, and though the Senate was in session, it was a rare day that a quorum of Senators were present.

Which was not to say that Lincoln's time went unused. He had discussions and negotiations nearly constantly, and almost all of them seemed designed to unsettle and upset him.

The cabal, at this point, began to make itself known. Not as a specific roster of people, but the existence of a movement to modify the United States in a manner that would make it unrecognizable. It was, it seemed, a movement to make the federal government subservient to those of the states, and specifically to those states of the South.

A fragment from Lincoln's diary:

Former Governor Gist requested a meeting with me, and for courtesy's sake, I granted it. Gist has been out of the government for several years, so I was unsure what he wanted.

Thus, I was surprised when he bustled into my office, sat down, and exuded the confidence of an ambassador negotiating a peace treaty.

*I was shocked when the first words out of his mouth were a demand—*demand*—that amounted to full-scale surrender. Certainly, he couched his demand in diplomatic terms. "Several amendments to update the Constitution, bring it into the modern world," he said, handing me a sheaf of papers. "I think they'll make the government more effective, more efficient, more representative of what the people want."*

I knew, even before I read his papers, that effectiveness and efficiency were not Mr. Gist's goal.

Those proposed amendments, as everyone now knows, would have been the emasculation of federal government in the United States, removing the last vestiges of central authority over the states. They resembled nothing so much as the original Articles of Confederation, but with a more explicit acceptance of slavery.

Needless to say, Lincoln did not approve.

In the first months of 1863—the last of the 37th Congress—the Southern Senators' former obstructionism turned to outright hostility. No longer were they content to merely stymie Lincoln's proposals, but now they began a campaign of active opposition to all Northern ideals. The Union's only salvation, at the time, was the presence of the seven previously missing Northern Senators, and the perfect attendance of every Northerner.

Gist continued to meet with Lincoln, but they both knew their sessions were futile, pro forma gatherings to give the appearance of ongoing negotiations.

At the same time, far from public view, Jefferson Davis was setting up his own shadow government, and preparing military options to compel Lincoln's acquiescence.

As the session sputtered to an end, the newly elected Senators were sworn in, but their presence merely served to exaggerate the dichotomy between Northerners and Southerners, and the first three weeks of the 38th Congress became unique for the legislature's inability to approve any legislation.

Lincoln's depression had returned, and with it, his physical infirmities. He looked forward to his trip home, yet he knew he'd be returning with his tail between his legs.

The Congress adjourned, and the Senators sped out of town.

Lincoln, however, was unable to join the exodus.

There is no record of the conversation that took place when Mr. Gist visited President Lincoln on March 15, 1863, the day after the Senate adjourned. John Hay—one of Lincoln's personal secretaries—reports what is known:

that Gist left the meeting with a spring in his step, and ashen-faced Lincoln called in Ward Hill Lamon for another closed-door session.

After Lamon left, Lincoln called in Hay and John Nicolay. As Hay recorded, "The President told us to gather our belongings, pull our hats down low, and hurry back to Illinois as quickly and quietly as possible."

While neither of Lincoln's secretaries would ordinarily think of questioning him, in this they presented a united front to oppose the President. "We wouldn't think of abandoning you," said Hay.

"No, sir," echoed Nicolay. "Unless you're coming with us, there is no way we can leave the capital."

The argument continued, but eventually, Lincoln told them Gist had threatened his life if he attempted to leave Columbia. "He is granting Mary and Tad safe passage home if I give my parole." At this time, Tad was a month shy of his tenth birthday, while Robert—nineteen years old—was at Harvard.

"Parole? Then this is war?"

To that, Lincoln offered no response, except to say he needed to confer with the Vice President immediately.

From *The Autobiography of Hannibal Hamlin*:

On March 15, 1863—the day after the Senate adjourned—I was sitting in my office, glumly mulling over the events of the last several weeks. My Senatorial duties were ended, and wouldn't pick up again for nine months. Based on the last two years, I knew that the time between Senate sessions left me with almost nothing to fill my official time, and I was again considering a trip home, and how best to explain my ineffectiveness to my neighbors.

Lincoln's aide, Nicolay, barged in breathlessly. "The President needs to see you," he said without preamble.

I followed Nicolay upstairs to Lincoln's office, expecting... I'm not sure what I was expecting, but such a peremptory summons was completely out of character.

I found him sitting calmly at his desk, a brooding expression on his face. Mentioning that expression reminds me that it wasn't something I would have remarked on, at the time, after the two years we'd been in Columbia.

Nicolay withdrew silently, and the President came right to the point.

"I'm a prisoner here. Gist has agreed to grant Mary and Tad safe passage home if I give my parole. If I don't... I'd rather not think about that. So I need you to leave, Mr. Vice President. Go home to Maine as if it were a standard vacation. But don't come back."

"Mr. President?"

"I need you outside the capital. This is a city under siege. They're not letting me out, and I feel certain they'll be cutting off my communications very soon, if they haven't already begun censoring them."

"What good will it do if I'm home in Maine?"

"You're the Vice President of the United States, Hannibal. I feel I'm going to need you to imitate your namesake."

"Find a herd of elephants and come marching over the Appalachians?"

"Something like that. Go home to Maine. Make it a public trip: the Senate has adjourned, so you're taking a vacation. Tell the public you're tired, and need to rest at home. Don't see anybody, don't give any interviews: go quiet. And then take a much more quiet, much more important trip. Visit as many of the Northern capitals as you can, and convince the state legislatures, the governors, and as many of the senators as you can find, that the South is in rebellion. The Constitution says the capital is here in Columbia for this decade, but it doesn't say the government has to do its work here. Tell the senators to stay out of the South. And tell the governors it's time to train up their militias."

"It'll look like a coup. I have no authority to call the government together."

"You're the President of the Senate. But you're right: trying to move the government into Maine will seem like a power grab."

"Somewhere else, then."

"Springfield, Hannibal, set up a government in Springfield."

"Then it will seem like your power grab, sir. Trying to move the government to your home state."

"I fear I'll never see Illinois again, Hannibal. I'm ill, but even that, of late, has become more remote in my thinking."

"Are you setting yourself up as a martyr, Mr. President?"

"I'm not hoping to, but it's feeling more and more as if that's the only road left open to me."

"We're not dead yet."

"No, and this may just be the wild imaginings of a frustrated, fevered mind. Nevertheless, I need you free and in the North. Gather the government, catch as many of the Supreme Court justices as you can, and tell Grant the training program we set up has to move double-time."

"Grant? That drunk?"

"Drunk when he's a civilian. But when he's in uniform, it does something to him. Ulysses Grant is the most brilliant strategist since... well, since that other Hannibal. I commissioned him last summer. You and [Secretary of War Edwin] Stanton will have to give him the full command, because we may have to attack the South to free the government."

"How will I know if it's time to cross that Rubicon? If they censor your communication..."

"It's coming to a head, Hannibal. If I don't send you a clear, unambiguous 'cease and desist' by the end of June, I'll have lost control of the situation. And if you don't hear anything from me, well, I'm probably dead, you're the President, and then it's all on your head."

From the diary of John Hay:

Sitting with the President as he watched Vice President Hamlin's entourage leave the capital today, I could feel the weight of the nation on his shoulders. He was stooped, morose, a man completely on his own.

> *Mrs. Lincoln and Tad left Columbia a few days ago, and Hamlin's departure was the last public event he had scheduled.*
>
> *He is still urging John and me to leave, but we discussed the situation, and decided that we're staying with him. He needs friendly faces and sympathetic ears, and while Mr. Lamon is here for the President's personal security, we will continue to help him keep the government operational.*

Following those departure ceremonies, Lincoln wasn't seen again in public. He continued to communicate via letters and wires, but no one outside his official "family" saw him. And many years later, Hay and Nicolay confirmed that the reports issued from the office of the President had indeed been tampered with, and were not Lincoln's own words, or, in many cases, even his own ideas.

Jefferson Davis later confirmed his own role in rewriting Lincoln's letters and wires. But he never admitted to holding Lincoln prisoner.

The assumption is that Gist, along with still unknown members of the cabal, handled that facet of the coup, for a coup it was, in deed if not in word.

Hay and Nicolay, too, were held in seclusion. They were allowed to see Lincoln, individually, infrequently, and never alone.

After two months of this house arrest, Lincoln eventually convinced Lamon that it was time to leave his side. Lamon never wrote of his experiences during this time, but it is known that Gist allowed him to leave

Columbia. He made his way north, and eventually to Vice President Hamlin's government in exile in Springfield. Hamlin later wrote that Lamon's arrival, more than anything else, convinced him that the tipping point had arrived, and that it was time to act.

At the same time Lincoln was convincing Lamon to leave, Hamlin was continuing his errand. After his public journey home, he stayed in Bangor for less than a day, before privately setting out on the 80-mile journey to Augusta, Maine, to confer with the governor of his home state. Leaving Augusta, Hamlin made a sub-rosa tour of the Northern state capitals. Such a grand effort, however, could not long be kept secret, and by the time he reached Columbus, Ohio, Hamlin had attracted such a following that he decided to go public.

"President Lincoln has charged me with preserving and protecting the Union. He is currently being held by forces intent on destroying our United States of America. Their aim is to take power for themselves, to extend slavery to free territories, and to make the federal government subservient to their local interests. This cannot be allowed.

"Therefore, in accordance with the President's wishes, I am heading to Illinois, Springfield to be exact, to convene the government there, and to determine—within the bounds of the Constitution—what we can do to maintain the nation and to free the President."

Standing with him for the speech, to show it wasn't a one-man show, were the Secretaries of State, the Treasury, War, and the Navy, whom Hamlin had met with on his trip West. Hamlin hadn't yet reached

Attorney General Bates—at home in Missouri—and Secretary of the Interior Usher (in Indiana). Postmaster General Blair, of Maryland, was assumed to have gone over to the South.

"I call on all Senators to join me in Springfield for an extraordinary session, to begin as soon as practicable.

"And I call on the Southern insurrectionists to reconsider their course of action, to free the President and accept the primacy of the Constitution. Join with us to heal the nation. Men of good conscience can disagree, but allowing that disagreement to rise to the level of a coup d'etat is wrong. I urge you to see the error of your ways, and reverse this course before any more damage is done."

As one might expect, Hamlin's speech was met with shocked silence and strong resolve… in the North.

In the South, he was called a traitor, and letters appeared, supposedly from the office of the President, firing the Cabinet and calling for the impeachment of Hamlin. Northern newspapers refused to print them.

Upon arriving in Springfield, and even before meeting with the Senate, Hamlin called for Grant, and they cloistered themselves in an office for several hours. As they later revealed, the sole purpose of that meeting was to plan the Northern attack on the South, with the twin aims of freeing the President and breaking the Southern will.

After making their plans, they met with the Cabinet and received unanimous approval. Then Lamon spoke up. As the last person to have seen Lincoln, who could most reliably report on the President's condition, Lamon was almost distraught in urging Hamlin and Grant to move up the schedule. "It is inconceivable that the President will live that long."

Unfortunately for Lincoln, Grant was a master strategist, and he knew there was no way the North could launch an attack in less than three months.

Grant went to organize the Army, and Hamlin sent for Allan Pinkerton, ordering him to plan a guerilla raid to free Lincoln.

The old animosity between Lamon and Pinkerton re-appeared. Lamon demanded the right to rescue Lincoln, but Pinkerton rightly pointed out that he had access to a larger, well-trained organization, where Lamon was but one man. Hamlin made his point stick through sheer force of will.

Pinkerton was able to sneak into the South, into Columbia, and into the Presidential apartment, but even as he was breaking in—disguised and unnoticed—he knew there was no way he'd be able to bring the President back out.

Nevertheless, Pinkerton was stunned when he snuck into the President's bedroom, and saw how drawn and ashen he was. "Mr. President?" he tremulously woke the once-great man. "The Vice President sent me to get you out."

"You look like a man who knows he can't do something. Mr…?"

"Pinkerton, sir. Allan Pinkerton. We met on the trip to your inauguration." Was Lincoln's mind going, too?

"Ah, yes, Mr. Pinkerton. I think you realize there's no way I can sneak out of Columbia. I'm so weak that I doubt I could even ride, let alone walk, to the city limits. I shall not see Illinois again."

Lincoln's symptoms lead Pinkerton to report, much later, that he assumed Lincoln was suffering a return bout of smallpox, or typhoid, or some sort of poisoning.

"No, sir, I don't think you will."

"What is Hamlin doing?"

"Following your orders, sir. Grant is in the field, but won't be ready for several months. That's why I was sent."

"You were sent to take me out of here, but if I die in the escape, nothing will be solved."

"What are you thinking, Mr. President?"

"I'm thinking that I'm a husk of the man I once was. There's not much else I can offer the world, except, perhaps, my death."

"Your death, sir?"

"My death. As a lonely pilgrim dying on the road, I am nothing. But as the President of the United States, murdered by a Southerner in a Southern capital, I may— just may—be a symbol of the importance of the Presidency, and of the changes that must be wrought on the government."

"Murdered, sir?"

"Murdered, Mr. Pinkerton. It's not so horrible to contemplate. At most, it will hasten my end by a few days. But if I can serve by my death… Find someone to do it. Make it a public spectacle. Let it embarrass my soi-disant hosts. Let my death be the rallying cry Hamlin needs to wrest control of the government from the petty, squabbling states."

Horrible as the idea was, Lincoln quickly won Pinkerton over to his way of thinking. "It will have to be in public. Not something hidden in this room, sir."

"Public, yes, public. Independence Day. Davis was in yesterday. The day before? Whichever. He said there's to be an Independence Day celebration, at which I am expected to appear. But he warned me against saying anything. Then. At that celebration. That's the time to do it."

"Sir, do you understand what you're saying? What you're asking me to do?"

"What I'm ordering you to do, Mr. Pinkerton. I'm ordering you to find some Southern patsy to murder me, and to loudly claim he did it for disunion. Don't let it be traced back to you."

"But your family?"

"My family. Poor, dear Mary. This will cause her great grief, but even without this plan, I will not see her again. I must ask something else of you, Mr. Pinkerton. When you get back to the North, be sure to tell her that my last thoughts were of her and the children. That I love her still. That I'm sorry I cannot be with her."

"I will, Mr. President."

"Then off with you, Mr. Pinkerton. Set it all up, and then get out of Columbia, out of South Carolina, as fast as you can."

As everyone knows now, Lincoln's plan was a success. But at the time, and for many years after, all we knew was that a middling-successful actor—who apparently had no idea what was really happening among the upper echelons of the government—had joined a conspiracy to decapitate it.

Photos of Lincoln at the Independence Day celebrations show him looking pained and drawn, sitting uncomfortably and resting on a cane. And yet, he also seems to be at peace, as if he knows what is coming, and the good that will come of it.

Of the actual moment, we have eyewitness reports: actor John Wilkes Booth approached the President from the back, pulled a pistol, shouted "Iura Australi," and shot Lincoln in the back of the head.

Even though Lincoln was surrounded by people one would assume wanted him dead, including Davis and Gist, the shock they all displayed at Booth's grisly act seemed both genuine and horrified.

In the bedlam that followed the gun shot, Booth was able to escape, and he ran.

The police caught up with him hours later, while he was holed up in a barn. Through shouted negotiations, Booth blamed a conspiracy, and demanded to know if Vice President Hamlin and Secretary of State Seward were also dead. Apparently, he was unaware that they weren't even in the South.

Eventually, Booth walked out of the barn with his hands in the air and no evidence of a weapon. There was much shouting, and several gun shots, and Booth died.

Many years later, on his death bed, Allan Pinkerton finally admitted killing John Wilkes Booth, and his role in the assassination of a President.

The National Archives then confirmed that President Hannibal Hamlin had issued a full—and secret—pardon to Pinkerton. "He never could thank me, because it was my action that made him President. But we both recognized the necessity of my acts for the greater good, the survival of the nation."

* * *

From the *Encyclopedia Americana*:

Following Lincoln's assassination, Hannibal Hamlin assumed the Presidency and, with Ulysses Grant in command of the Army, the Union forces managed to smash the South's defensive blockade, and bring Lincoln's body home. They also captured Jefferson Davis, William Gist, and the other leaders of the Southern uprising, thus ending the Great Schism.

The Senate refused to meet again in Columbia, and, in concert with Hamlin and the Cabinet, demanded a new, neutral site for the government. A commission was appointed, which decided the best course would be to carve out a capital territory, a District of Lincoln, on the border between the North and South. A suitable location was found, an unoccupied parcel of land straddling the Ohio River bordering Northern state Illinois and Southern state Kentucky (centered at 37.5 degrees North, 88.1 degrees West). Both states donated the land for what would come to be known as the capital city, Washington, D.L.

President Hamlin was elected to his own term in 1864, with the Southern states not partici-pating. By late 1865, the war was over, the Schism healed, and the South brought to heel.

The capitulating South agreed to the 13th and 14th Amendments, ending slavery and setting out a plan for a permanent, extraterritorial national capital in Washington, District of Lincoln.

President Hamlin spent the remainder of his term overseeing the construction of the capital city from temporary quarters in Springfield, and agitating for a stronger centralized government.

In the election of 1868, General Ulysses Grant was easily elected President.

Allan Pinkerton founded a security and investigation firm, but he wore a haunted expression for the rest of his days.

How I Won the Lottery, Broke the Time Barrier (or is that "Broke the Time Barrier, Won the Lottery"), and Still Wound Up Broke

(first published in
Analog Science Fiction and Fact, June 2000)

I didn't plan to write so many stories having to do with time travel in its various incarnations; it just sort of happened that way. This is one of those. And you can probably guess which day the idea came to me.

I'm sitting at my desk at home reading *Physics Review Letters* (you read your romantic thrillers, I'll read mine), and I hear a loud pop, followed by the sound of wind rushing past my right ear.

A voice, sort of like mine, says "Listen carefully. I'm from your future. For me, today is March 16th, 2026. For you, it's March 16th, 1999. Tomorrow's Lotto drawing is for forty-five million dollars. The winning numbers will be 17, 19, 30, 32, 42, and 51."

I decide to play along. "Why are you telling me?" But I hedge my bet—I always read with a pen and paper, so I write down the numbers.

"Because you're me, and this is your destiny."

The rushing sound stops with a loud pop.

What the hell—I'm broke. I know I'm capable of great things, if I could only get far enough ahead, financially, to get out of my dead-end job, but being an introverted lab assistant at a minor university is not a high-growth position. I buy a ticket. *It came to me in a dream* will be as good an explanation as any other.

I win. $45,000,000, payable in 26 annual installments. Call it $800,000 a year, after taxes.

That's enough to go into full-time research.… I'm no fool—if I'm going to communicate with myself in the past, I'm going to have to build a time machine. At the same time, it's also not something eager young lab assistants talk seriously about—better to do the research in secret.

I go from nearly broke to living like a pauper with a hobby that costs three quarters of a million dollars a year. Books, studying, conferences, research, and increasingly more expensive equipment.

Keeping the project a secret isn't too hard—I've always kept to myself—but it does mean post office boxes for my subscriptions and mail orders, and attending those conferences with different names—always as an anonymous attendee, never as a participant.

Ten years of research, and I'm making some real progress. For instance, I now know it will be much easier to build a machine that only needs to traverse the time barrier, without having to move in space. That means my best bet is to build it right here, in the very bedroom/office in which I received the message.

Well, my landlord decides to sell the building out from under me, and suddenly, I'm about to lose the spacial congruence that seems necessary to success.

I find myself a lawyer, and get him to negotiate with the landlord.

The negotiations go well: to cover the mortgage, the bank will take my next six annual Lotto payments. I convince them to leave me living expense money, and they make it almost all of the next eight payments. And, of course, I'll have to hire a superintendent.

I can continue my study undisturbed, but physical research will have to wait until I can again afford new equipment. It's amazing how you forget how much you need $750,000 a year until you don't have it.

Things are finally starting to look plausible. The energy source will cost me two million dollars—three years' payments—and with that much juice flowing through it, the equipment will destroy itself after one use. But it can be done.

Everything's ready, but for the power. I'm forced back to inactivity, to save my last three payments to buy the power source, but I persevere.

Finally, the big day. The machine is ready to open a small, short-duration, 27-year-long artificial wormhole. I drink some water to make sure my voice is clear, sit next to the aperture, and power up.

There are a few bangs and pops, something that looks like lightning, and an infinitely long tunnel of fog appears in the aperture.

Remembering those 27-year-old prophetic words, I say "Listen carefully. I'm from your future. For me, today is March 16th, 2026. For you, it's March 16th, 1999. Tomorrow's Lotto drawing is for forty-five million dollars. The winning numbers will be 17, 19, 30, 32, 42, and 51."

A younger, far-away (and long-ago) voice comes back to me: "Why are you telling me?"

I guess I was a bit of a skeptic back then. "Because you're me, and this is your destiny." I'm glad I've been able to remember the conversation all these years—I don't even want to think about the paradox of saying something different.

The fog flows away as the bangs get louder, and the lightning dimmer. Then there's a final loud bang and blackness.

The next thing I know, I'm lying against the far wall, behind an overturned lab bench. The only light comes from holes in the wall… and the dying flames of my equipment under the sprinkler system.

The paramedics check me out and declare me fit. The fire department checks my building out and condemns it.

Now what? I've created, used, and destroyed a single-use time machine. I've spent 27 years and my entire fortune to build and use it, ensuring that I'll have won that Lotto jackpot. The greatest scientific achievement of generations, and if I talk about it, the only thing I'll get is ridicule. "You expect me to believe that you won forty-five million dollars, and then spent it all to ensure that you'd win it, and incidentally, destroyed the proof that you built a time machine? Yeah, right. You're only trying to justify losing an entire fortune."

I wonder if my old lab assistant position is still available.

Fermat's Legacy

(first published in
Analog Science Fiction & Fact, September 1992)

This is my first professionally published story. I'd been submitting stories to all the major science fiction magazines for years, and started working as the editorial assistant at Analog *(and* Asimov's*) in 1989. But even as an employee, I kept getting rejection letters. One day in late 1991, a day Stanley Schmidt (*Analog's *editor) was in the office, he stuck his head in my office and said, "So, was Pierre de Fermat married?" I realized I hadn't done all my research, and on my lunch break, ran to the main branch of the New York Public Library (four blocks from the office), found a biographical encyclopedia which had a listing for Fermat, and discovered that he had indeed been married. I photocopied the page, went back to the office, and showed it to Stan. He said, "Hmm. Then I guess I'll buy your story." I think that was the first time he'd gotten a hug for buying a story.*

It was the winter of 1662, and Pierre de Fermat was a very angry old man. "Dammit," he cried, throwing the book across the room. "I came up with that theory first!"

"Which theory was that, dear?" Mme. Fermat solicitously picked up the book and brought it back to him.

"The calculus. I discovered the method of tangents, but does anyone say, 'Oh, Fermat, what a mathematician'? No!

It's always Newton, Newton, Newton. Damn that Englishman!"

"Now Pierre, you know it's not Mr. Newton's fault. Why don't you take a nap?"

By this time, Fermat was really going. "What about analytic geometry? I did that too. But all they say is, 'Well, Descartes did most of the same work.' Descartes! He's nothing but a lousy philosopher!"

"Please, Pierre, Rene is a very nice philosopher. You're getting yourself worked up over nothing."

"Over nothing? How about probability theory? Pascal and I did a lot of that work together. But who gets invited to speak at all the scientific congresses? Who gets invited to lecture at all the universities? Not me!"

"Please, dear, remember your charity to your fellow man. The judge of history will win out, and you'll be remembered as the great mathematician you are. After all, you and I know you've done all that work. History will have to remember you for all you've done."

A light appeared in Fermat's eye, but his wife didn't notice--she thought her words had finally gotten through.

In a way, they had.

Fermat ran into his study and slammed the door. "History will remember me," he muttered. "I'll show them. If they won't accept my genius while I'm alive, then let them puzzle over it after I am gone."

But how to do it? How to so turn the world upside down that his name would be remembered forever, without appearing to have done so purposely?

Fermat pulled volumes from the shelves, paging through them furiously, and tossing each aside as he reached for the next. Finally, his eye passed over a reference to the Pythagorean Theorem, and he laughed. "That's it! If they won't remember me for what I've done, let them remember me for what I haven't done."

He stumbled through the pile of books on the floor to his desk, grabbed a quill and dipped it, and, in the margin, scrawled: "$x^n + y^n = z^n$ no solution when n (integer) > 2. Wonderful proof, no room. Note to me: WRITE OUT THE PROOF."

Fermat lived three more years, and was much more pleasant. He was generally happier, although less driven... except that he was constantly calculating equations, and then throwing the papers into the fire.

And Fermat made sure never to loan that book to anyone.

In June 1993, Andrew Wiles gave a lecture in which he described solving the proof. In August, a flaw was pointed out to him. Late in 1994, he found the solution, and in May 1995, published the 129-page paper proving the theorem. However, much of the math and techniques in the proof were unknown in Fermat's time.

A Glance Backward

(first published in *Analog Science Fiction and Fact*,
September 1993)

*Making my first professional fiction sale did not
suddenly make the process any easier. The floodgates did
not open to a steady stream of acceptances. Indeed, it
took another year to make my second sale. This is also
the first of my time travel-ish stories.*

Tom, from Paleontology, plops himself into my guest
chair.

"You look beat, Tom."

"You try solving a 65 million-year-old mystery and
see how you look after a while."

I know I look much happier than Tom. I'm wearing an
idiot grin and drinking champagne out of a paper cup.

Tom looks at my face, and his scowl deepens. "So, tell
me," he growls.

I tell him. Twenty minutes ago we finally succeeded
in capturing and stabilizing a wormhole for a few seconds
in the physics lab. Actually, we'd caught one end of it in
the lab. The other, as near as we could tell, was about four
minutes in the past out around Mars. But we'd kept it and
even widened it a bit.

"I don't get it," he rumbles. Tom is not a polymath.

"Do you even know what a wormhole is?" I ask.

"Something a worm leaves in the dirt?"

"A wormhole," I say in my best lecture voice, "is a
tunnel, spontaneously formed by quantum fluctuations,
that sometimes persists after its formation, and that

connects two otherwise unconnected points in space-time."

"What?"

"It's a tunnel through space and time."

"Hey, that's great," Tom brightens. "Can you let me take a look at Earth 65 million years ago—to see what happened to the dinosaurs?"

"It doesn't work that way," I explain. "We don't make wormholes. We use what we can find. The two ends get separated in time when one accelerates and the other doesn't. The greater the separation, the less chance we have of finding one, and 65 million years is a long time."

"Well, work on it," Tom says. "It might be the thing to get me my doctorate."

That's a sore spot. We're both grad students, but I'm in a new field, where finding something new to work on, like wormholes, is easy. Paleontology's kind of old—harder to find a thesis topic in.

"I'll work on it," I say. "But the longest wormhole we've found so far was about 27 minutes, and we couldn't hold on to it. If we could get more powerful magnets, and a better generator, maybe we'd have a better chance."

"I'll see what I can do," Tom says. He's always been a good scrounger.

Four months later, Tom's helped get us a huge combined grant from the NSF—combining the studies of wormholes and paleontology. We've got money to throw at all the equipment we could want.

We find a wormhole something like 100 years long, and we're actually able to hold on to it for three hours—long enough to realize we can steer the other end… a little.

Tom's in the lab, but he seems really down amongst our elation.

"What?" I ask.

"Only 100 years? That's nothing. We need 65 million."

I shake my head and walk away.

A year later, we've been having more success. We've got a wormhole that goes back about 2,000 years—the other end was somewhere in the Oort Cloud when we found it—and we saw the nova that led the three... well, you know.

Anyway, we've been able to steer the other end in toward the planets—really slowly, but it's amazing what you can do with a good particle accelerator and all the money you can use. When science connects to "real world" interests, grants flow like water (of course, the Church's little donation didn't hurt either).

Tom somehow convinced the university to give him his doctorate, even though we still haven't been able to find a wormhole back to the K-T... multi-million-year-old wormholes are not that common.

The grant money's slowing down. Everyone's seen the pictures of the universe a few million years ago and it's getting hard to make the spectacular discoveries that grab headlines and funding.

Tom's in town for a paleontology conference. "You're getting a little gray," he says.

"You're no spring chicken, either," I respond. It seems this has been our opening for years.

"Still haven't figured out what happened to my dinosaurs, have you?"

A grad student runs into my office. "Doctor, come quick. We've got a long one."

"How long?" I ask. I'm getting jaded in my old age.

"Dr. Stewart isn't sure. On the order of 60 million years or so."

Tom's eyes sparkle as he jumps up.

We get to the lab as Stewart is saying "...old. About 66 million years. It's definitely
Earth. See the different continents?"

"And where's the other end?" I ask.

"About half a million kilometers off the surface. Hey! That looks like another moon! Smaller. I'm steering the hole for a better look."

I glance through. "Stewart, it's coming this way—"

"Tell me, Gurrgh," says Khggah, thumping his tail, "what do you think killed the trilobites?"

"I don't know," Gurrgh says, looking up into the sky and seeing the smaller moon disappear. The ground starts to tremble.

The Ears Have It

(first published in
Analog Science Fiction and Fact, December 1993)

Analog divides the stories it publishes by length: serialized novels, novellas, novelettes, and short stories. The magazine also has an occasional feature story called Probability Zero, which is 1,000 words or fewer, usually about an idea which—at first glance—makes sense, although further consideration points out how absurd it is. Most of my sales to Analog *have been Probability Zeroes.*

This, my third sale (my third Probability Zero), made me eligible to join the Science Fiction Writers of America. I'd been involved with the organization (which has changed its name several times since then, though it retains the SFWA acronym) through my work at Analog *and* Asimov's*, so joining didn't reveal to me any great secrets (actually, the organization didn't have any), but it was a significant milestone in my mind. At the time, in order to be eligible to join, one had to have one professional novel publication or three professionally published short stories. This story—and the two before it—were my qualification. Combined, they total 2,000 words, which I think may have been the smallest word count anyone had used to join the organization.*

"Earth can't be the only one. There must be other intelligences out there. If not precisely like us, at least close enough that we could communicate. We have to try to find them."

"What do you suggest?"

"Well, it seems logical to me to assume that being intelligent, they'd be trying to contact others, as we are. In fact, they probably already are. They'd probably try to communicate electromagnetically, and it would probably be with radio waves. We ought to build a huge receiver, and then keep listening...."

"We have become sterile, Preco!ng, insular. Our ideas no longer grow because we each know the others' thoughts. We need more contact. We need to talk with beings who have different backgrounds."

"And where, Kruny!tk, do you think we might find these beings whose backgrounds differ so widely from our own?"

"Out among the stars. Lo!thar!el can't be the only planet to have evolved intelligent life."

"And what do you suggest we do?"

"We must have such contact soon, or we'll stagnate and die. If we begin transmitting a signal now, by the time it reaches the stars, and the star-beings are able to answer, it may be too late. We should, instead, listen as intently as possible...."

"But Zgorph, we are astronologers! We have long held dear the belief that life did not originate on Zzqolin alone. I put it to you that now is the time to prove that."

"How do you propose we go about proving it?"

"We must make contact with those otherworldly life-forms. We must communicate with them. Perhaps we ought to signal that we are here. I think a high-powered transmission of radio waves in some basic code to signal our presence would suffice to start."

"And how much would this high-powered radio transmitter cost? You know as well as I that the astronomy budget has been decimated this past decade, and even low-powered radio transmitters have been rising in cost. Have you a cheap idea?"

"Well, I suppose we could instead build a receiver, and listen for such signals."

"Now you're speaking sense...."

"Do you really think the Overseer will allow us to embark on such a difficult project as trying to talk to the stars? Scurrying around, sending signals, varying the means and directions of transmission? You heard her talk last week, saying that V'schuntlik would be a better place if it were a simpler place."

"Do you think the Overseer would allow a project to listen to the stars? Surely that is a simple thing."

"Perhaps, perhaps. I have an appointment with the Third Assistant Underseer next week. I will broach the topic then...."

"We are recovering from the most devastating war ever. The war to finally unify all of Qu-shon, and now you want to use large amounts of money and effort to try to find extra-Qu-shonian life? Do you think the people would go for that?"

"I don't see why not."

"You don't see why not? What if your extra-Qs come and attack us? Everyone is tired from years of wars, and you want to invite more. You want to call some extra-Q intelligence, which can travel the stars, and have it come kill us?"

"Well, perhaps that isn't such a good idea. But if they're out there, oughtn't we at least find out so that we'll be able to prepare ourselves in case they find us on their own? Maybe passively listen for them?"

"Hmm. I may be able to convince the Budget Council of the utility of that suggestion...."

"Earth is now ready to take its place among the intelligences in the galaxy. We have active search programs taking place at Arecibo and the Very Large Array in the California desert. We're bound to pick up an extra-terrestrial signal any time now...."

"...Kruny!tk, you have your wish. Lo!thar!el now has listening stations all about its equatorial belt. If there are other beings out there, we will soon find them, and will be safe from stagnation...."

"...We've managed to have enough funds assigned the astronologers to build a receiver, Zornack. If there are indeed otherworldly life-forms, Zzqolin will soon know...."

"...I am surprised, but the Overseer thinks that listening to the stars will not harm V'schuntlik's way of life. She said we could being the project immediately...."

"...The Ruling Council has decided that listening for extra-Qu-shonian life is the most prudent course for Qu-shon. Accordingly, listening posts will be established...."

Earth listened intently.

Lo!thar!el listened intently.

* * *

Zzqolin listened intently.

V'schuntlik listened intently.

Qu-shon listened intently.

Nobody said anything.

Without An S
(first published in
Analog Science Fiction and Fact, November 1995)

After selling stories #2 and #3, I went back to my old ways of earning rejection after rejection. It got a bit frustrating. But I kept at it. Another thing to note is that Analog *has a long history of publishing recursive stories; stories in which the magazine or its staff feature. This is the first of my three recursive* Analog *stories.*

A friend of mine, author Michael A. Burstein, made his first sale to the magazine while I was the associate editor. I called to tell him the good news. His second story was another one of the recursive Probability Zero stories, turning me into a character.

It started with The Rejection Letter (which, I suppose, seems backward, but then… well, keep reading).

Anyway, The Letter read, in full: "Dear Ian, I liked this story, but I'm afraid I have to reject it because of a matter of timelines. I bought one fairly similar to it the week before yours arrived. It isn't close enough that you should worry about sending it elsewhere, but it is too close for me to publish both in *Analog*."

But I wanted it to be in *Analog*! I reread the rejection letter a little more closely.

Now that I look back on the whole thing—in a retrospect which can be mine alone—the last word in the first sentence probably was a typo, but when I got the letter (which won't happen now), I read it as written. Timelines, rather than timeliness with an S.

That's when I decided to rewrite the story, adding another timeline. It came out, I feel, much better than the original. I have no real way of knowing if Stan thinks it's better, since after the rewrite he'll never see my original version.

Anyway, I rewrote it, and put it in the back of a file drawer. My room is always a mess, so I had no fear of anyone else finding the original version, the new version, or the rejection letter. I put it in the drawer, let it languish, and proceeded to make enough money to fund a little research. Yes, you've probably figured out what type, after all this *is* a science fiction magazine.

I stepped into the time machine, traveled back to a time some two weeks before this story started, and handed myself the new version of the as-yet unwritten story.

I'd lived with science fiction so long that my younger self didn't seem much surprised by my arrival. I/he took the brand new story on now-yellowed paper, retyped and submitted it. Now you know where the early part of this narrative comes from.

Seeing what I look like in his future must have been kind of strange, but I/he can handle it. How's that saying go? Reality is for people who can't handle science fiction?

Anyway, having a good memory, I, as usual, didn't bother to bring back-up material. And that's the only thing I regret in this little incident—the younger me will never see the original, because I didn't bring it along. I/he'll never know what story will have prompted The Rejection Letter which in turn prompted this story.

If only Stan could handle timelines like his letter suggested, perhaps he could tell me....

Living It Is the Best Revenge
(first published in
Analog Science Fiction and Fact, February 1996)

*With this sale, I was finally able to break out of the Probability Zero ghetto, and publish a full-fledged short story. The cover date matched my last days working for the magazine; I left after six years to start my own magazine (*Artemis Magazine, *which ran from 2000 to 2003).*

At the end of each year, Analog *takes a poll of its readers to award the Analytical Laboratory [readers' choice] Awards. In the spring of 1997, I was stunned to learn that "Living It Is the Best Revenge" had won the AnLab for Best Short Story of 1996. It was a double-shocker: my fact article, "The Coming of the Money Card: Boon or Bane?" (which appeared in the October 1996 issue) won the AnLab for Best Fact Article.*

Mark was walking to the subway station at a brisk pace. It was late, and he wanted to get home.

The sidewalks were wet from the rain, but fortunately, it had stopped before he left the office, since he'd forgotten to bring—

His back was on fire!

Then he felt cold as ice.

He dropped his brief case, and felt the sidewalk rush up at him. Then a hand rolled him over onto his back, and he saw a shaggy young man with a bandanna tied over his nose and mouth. The young man was holding a shiny black knife.

Mark tried to say something, but his mouth wouldn't work.

The young man checked each pocket, removed Mark's wallet and started to walk away. Then he stopped, turned back, and wiped the bloody knife on Mark's jacket.

Mark moaned in pain, and tried to call for help.

The sound of footsteps brought him back to himself.

The woman screamed, and the man hurried out of sight. He returned moments later and said, "Lie still. An ambulance is coming. You're going to be all right."

Mark's first ambulance ride was a confusion of sights and sounds as he faded into and out of consciousness. The paramedic stabbing his arm with a needle. The siren. The ambulance lurching from side to side. The paramedic screaming "Faster, Joe! He won't hang on much longer!"

Then the flickering of light and not light in his eyes as he was wheeled into and through a hospital. Then, a black gas mask came down over his face.

"Mark, can you hear me?" Ginny's face was tired and streaked with tears. Her hair was messed—mussed, she would say—and she was sniffling as she held his hand to her chest.

"Ginny," he said, or tried to say.

"I'm here, honey. I'm here. I was so worried."

"Ginny, I'm very tired."

"Of course you are, darling. You rest. I'll stay right here."

"Mr. Taylor? I'm Dr. Schoenfeld. I'm the one who operated on you last night. This is Detective Morrow."

"What am I doing here?"

"Do you remember anything about last night," Morrow asked.

He turned his head, and saw Ginny holding his hand. She looked like she'd been up all night.

"I was working late in the office. I was walking to the subway, and glad it had stopped raining, because I'd forgotten my umb…"

"And then what."

"Then, then… I… felt this incredible pain in my back. It was like I was burning up, and then freezing, and I fell down."

"Yes?"

"And a… a man… with a bandanna on his face… holding a knife, he took my wallet."

"Do you think you'd recognize this man, Mr. Taylor?"

"I… I don't know. It was dark, and I wasn't thinking too clearly, and… could I have a drink of water, please?"

"Of course, Mr. Taylor. Detective, please don't tire him out. Mr. Taylor's going to be with us for a few days, yet."

"Doctor, we're holding a man right now. We think he's the man who attacked Mr. Taylor. But if we can't officially charge him with anything, we'll have to release him soon. If Mr. Taylor could swear a complaint, we'd have sufficient grounds to hold him."

"All right, Detective. What do you need me to say?"

A nurse was whispering with Dr. Schoenfeld by the door.

"What is it, Doctor?"

"You seem to be having a reaction to something, Mr. Taylor. We're not quite sure why you still have a fever."

He had been feeling worse today, rather than better. Mark started to feel nauseous again, and reached for the barf bucket barely in time.

When he stopped heaving, and had rinsed his mouth, the doctor said, "We're going to have do some blood tests."

Mark held out his arm resignedly, as the nurse returned with a needle and some test tubes.

Mark was shivering and his whole body ached, as Ginny brought the kids in to see him.

"Daddy, Daddy," five-year-old Maggie cried, as she saw him lying there. "You have to get up. You have to get better. You promised!"

Mark Junior, who was twelve, was more reserved, but in his eyes, Mark could see the fear of death. It made him shiver even more.

"Ginny," Mark mumbled.

"I'm here, honey," she replied, patting his hand.

"I'm so tired, babe," he barely whispered.

"Then sleep, Mark, sleep. It's okay, I'll be right here."

"Okay," he said, and faded into unconsciousness.

"Did the prisoner know he was going to experience this?"

"The State Supreme Court allowed our experiments, but said we could only try the system on volunteers, and that if a psychological interview after the treatment agrees with our assessment, commutation of their sentences would be possible. Ethically, we decided we also needed the permission of the victims. In this case, Ginny gave permission. Of course, all the emotions and feelings may not be precisely what they felt at the time… in some cases we've had to make best guesses, but overall, the feeling is close, and the results are quite good."

"So after he's experienced the death of Mark…?"

"Then he'll experience the grief of his loss as felt by Ginny, and by Mark Junior, and by Maggie, and everyone else involved."

"Mrs. Taylor?" It was a voice that sounded like bad news.

"Yes?"

"My name is Dr. Schoenfeld. I'm at City Hospital. Your husband was just brought in, and… well… I think you should be here."

"Oh my god!" Ginny screamed. "What happened?"

"Please, Mrs. Taylor, it will be easier to explain in person."

"I'm on my way."

"Judy? It's Ginny. I know it's late, but I have to bring the kids over. The hospital just called. Mark's there, but they wouldn't say why. No, I'm not okay. I need you to take the kids so I can go. We're on our way.

"Come on kids," Ginny said, as she helped them put their jackets on over their pajamas. "You're going to stay with Sam and Joanne. I have to go see Daddy."

"But why, Mommy?" asked Maggie.

"Because he fell and hurt himself, and now he's in the hospital. I'm going to go get him, and bring him home. But it may take a while, so you're going to sleep at Sam and Joanne's house. Now come on, we have to get going." *Move it!* she wanted to scream, but she couldn't. It hurt to lie to them, but she had to get to the hospital *now*.

* * *

Ohgod, ohgod, ohgod!

Mark's been hurt!

He's dying!

He's *dead!*

Gotta get there, gotta get there, gotta get there.

The red and blue flashing lights in the mirror made Ginny slow down. *No!* her mind screamed, *Mark needs me!*

"Do you know how fast you were go—"

"My husband's in the hospital! He needs me! I have to get there! Please, I have to get there *now!* They just called! Please!"

"All right, all right. Slow down, lady. I'll let you off with a warning, this time. But don't go speeding, or you'll be a patient, too."

"Thank you." She rolled up her window, and tried not to speed away.

"My husband. I have to see him."

"Excuse me, ma'am. Are you all right?"

"My husband! You called, said he was here."

"Who called? What's your husband's name?"

"Mark. Mark Taylor. My husband's name is Mark. Dr. Schoenfeld called me and said I had to get to the hospital. Had to be here."

"All right, Mrs. Taylor. Have a seat over there, and I'll see if I can find Dr. Schoenfeld."

"I have to see Mark *now!*"

"I'll go get Dr. Schoenfeld, Mrs. Taylor."

"Mrs. Taylor, your husband was stabbed. He came through surgery just fine, and he's in the recovery room at the moment. We couldn't wait for permission to operate, but there are some forms we need—"

"I don't care about forms. I have to see Mark!"

"As I said, Mrs. Taylor, he's in the recovery room. He should be there for a few more hours. After he wakes up, we'll take him to a room, and you can stay with him."

"But I have to see him!" Why couldn't this doctor understand? Why couldn't anyone understand? She had to see Mark now! To make sure he was okay.

He looked so weak, so fragile. Laying there with tubes stuck in his arms, and wires attached to his chest. Her cheeks felt wet, and her vision blurred. *Why wouldn't he wake up?*

She was so tired, sitting here holding his hand. So tired, but so wired. She couldn't even think about sleeping. She had to watch Mark, make sure he was going to be okay.

Why wouldn't he wake up? The doctor said he'd be asleep for a while, but he didn't say how long a while.

She glanced at her watch, then out the window. It was getting light. Have to call Judy soon, she thought, and have her help the kids get to school. Explain to them on the phone.

"Why me? Why him? Why *us?*" she sobbed softly.

His eyes were fluttering. Maybe he was waking up. "Mark? Mark? It's me. Mark, wake up!" His eyes stayed closed.

"Mark, can you hear me?"

Finally, his eyes opened, and seemed to focus on her. His lips moved, and he seemed to be saying "Ginny."

The fist that had been squeezing her chest since Dr. Schoenfeld called finally released its grip.

"I'm here, honey. I'm here. I was so worried." *How dare you let yourself get hurt like that!* she wanted to scream.

"Ginny, I'm very tired." His eyes started to close again.

"Of course you are, darling. You rest. I'll stay right here. I won't let anybody hurt you again. I'll be here, you rest."

He was already asleep.

"Judy? It's Ginny. Mark's going to be okay. He was stabbed. I'm with him now. I'm calling from the phone in his room. He woke up a few minutes ago, and recognized me, and then went back to sleep. Look, I have to stay with him. Can you get the kids to school? Thanks. Tell them something?"

The doctor walked into the room, followed by a small man in a brown suit. The small man was holding a notebook and a pen.

"Mr. Taylor? I'm Dr. Schoenfeld. I'm the one who operated on you last night. This is Detective Morrow."

"What am I doing here?" Mark's voice was weak, but recognizable.

"Do you remember anything about last night?" Morrow asked.

What are you doing here asking questions? Ginny wanted to yell at him. *Go find the bastard who did this!*

He turned his head, and saw Ginny holding his hand.

He looked so small and weak. *What happened to the big, strong man who went to work yesterday morning?*

"I was working late in the office. I was walking to the subway, and glad it had stopped raining, because I'd forgotten my umb…"

"And then what."

What were they talking about? Mark was lying here with a hole in his back, and this detective wanted to know about his walk to the subway?

"Then, then… I… felt this incredible pain in my back. It was like I was burning up, and then freezing, and I fell down."

"Yes?"

"And a… a man… with a bandanna on his face… holding a knife, he took my wallet."

"Do you think you'd recognize this man, Mr. Taylor?"

"I… I don't know. It was dark, and I wasn't thinking too clearly, and… could I have a drink of water, please?"

"Of course, Mr. Taylor. Detective, please don't tire him out. Mr. Taylor's going to be with us for a few days, yet."

"Doctor, we're holding a man right now. We think he's the man who attacked Mr. Taylor. But if we can't officially charge him with anything, we'll have to release him soon. If Mr. Taylor could swear a complaint, we'd have sufficient grounds to hold him."

"All right, Detective. What do you need me to say?"

He'd been lying there, shivering, not getting any stronger. Maybe showing him the kids will help, she thought, and went to the waiting room.

"Come on, kids, we're going to go see Daddy. Remember what I said: he's been hurt, and he's not feeling very good, so he looks kind of sick, and he's very weak." Maggie's eyes were huge, and Mark Junior looked angry. "He's going to be okay, but he's going to be in the hospital for a while."

She knew that if she said it enough, believed it enough, it would happen. It *had* to happen. Mark *would* get better!

Mark was shivering, but his mouth smiled they walked in. He would get better; she knew it.

"Daddy, Daddy," Maggie cried, as she saw him lying there. "You have to get up. You have to get better. You promised!"

"Now, Maggie, remember what I told you," Ginny admonished. "He will get better, but he has to rest for a while.

Mark Junior was more reserved.

"Ginny," Mark mumbled. His eyes didn't open.

"I'm here, honey," she replied, patting his hand. It felt cold and weak.

"I'm so tired, babe." She struggled to hear him.

"Then sleep, Mark, sleep. It's Okay, I'll be right here." *And I'll kill anyone who tries to hurt you!*

"Okay," he said, and faded into unconsciousness.

An hour later, he stopped breathing. Ginny wasn't sure at first, but then an alarm went off, and a nurse came running.

Ginny looked at her face, and screamed in pain.

"Come on Mark, you have to wake up."

It was dark as Mom shook his shoulder. He rubbed his eyes and looked at her.

"Why, Mom? Is it time to go to school already?"

"No. Daddy was hurt. I have to go to the hospital to be with him. You and Maggie are going to stay with Sam and Joanne. Come on, you don't have to get dressed. Just put on your sneakers, and put your coat on over your pajamas."

"You see, the perpetrator is going to live, through our Live-It™ system, the lives of each of his victims. He'll experience all the feelings of every person who suffered for his crime."

"And when he's finished?"

"When he's gone through each of them—in this case, that means Mark, the victim, his wife, his two children, both his parents and his in-laws, and his business partner—then we run him through a simulation where he is himself with the same opportunity he had when he committed the crime. If he commits it again, we run him through the whole cycle again.

"And he keeps living through all their lives until there is some change in him."

"And if there is no change?"

"Then this will amount to a life-imprisonment. Life as a victim of a stabbing and robbery, over and over again."

"And do you think he'll be here for life?"

"Oh, no. Most of the young criminals, early in their careers, that we've tested the system on, are usually turned from a life of crime after two or three repetitions."

It was cold and dark, and the wind was blowing through his thin coat. He shivered. At least the bandanna over his nose and mouth kept a little warmth in, and holding the handle of the knife in his pocket was a comfort.

A man was walking toward him. A man in a suit and warm-looking overcoat, carrying a briefcase. He was hurrying, and the sound of his shoes on the pavement was almost like dog toenails on tile.

It was so cold, and he was so hungry. He needed some money for food, and maybe for a better coat, or a place to stay. The suit looked like he had plenty. Surely it wouldn't hurt to ask him for some.

Of course, moving that fast, the suit would never stop for him. But he had the knife…

Then he thought of the suit's—no, not the suit's, the *person's*—wife and kids and family. Was it really worth that man's life for the few bucks in his pocket?

"Hey, mister," Tommy called out to him, "You know where the homeless shelter is?"

On the Rocks

(first published in *Analog Science Fiction and Fact*, January/February 2022)

As I said earlier, one of the defining characteristics of a Probability Zero story is that, at first glance, it could happen. But when you think about it, the probability of it actually occurring is… well… zero. It's the type of fiction I like reading and writing.

You've heard of "two truths and one lie," right? Let me tell you about "two true memories and one false memory." At least, that's the reality of it, though someone else telling you my story would tell you it's "how I saved humanity from global warming."

I'll give you the three right here, and you can decide which is false: one was a memory of a high school chemistry class, one was a story from 1952, and one was a story from 1993. I know, that's not enough to go on. Try this: Isaac Asimov's "The Martian Way" talked about the residents of Mars traveling to Saturn to mine the ice in the rings for water and rocket fuel. Doug Beason's "To Bring Down the Steel" was about bringing metallic asteroids to Earth and floating them in the atmosphere. My chemistry teacher said something about the atmosphere being (at least functionally) a liquid.

Don't shout out the answer now. It doesn't really matter. What mattered was that I had those three memories, and didn't know one was false. I had those three memories, and I had more money than any one person needs… no, that's not right. Since the result is that

I saved the world, apparently I had as much money as one person needed to save humanity.

I had those memories, I had the money, and I knew we were in trouble due to global warming. I was thinking about it one warm evening, holding a drink, listening to the ice cubes clink in it as I fiddled with the glass. And that's when I had the breakthrough.

My thinking went like this:

When my drink is too warm, I put in ice cubes, and it cools down. My drink is liquid.

Global warming says the planet is too warm, because the atmosphere is getting warmer. The atmosphere can be considered a liquid.

So we need to cool down the atmosphere. And the obvious solution is to add ice cubes.

Sure, it sounds crazy to you now, reading this after the fact. But remember, at the time, it didn't sound crazy to me. And since I was the guy with the money, it was a workable theory.

I knew enough about the concept of a "closed system" to know that we couldn't just take ice from the poles and throw it up into the atmosphere. I knew we'd need to get ice from somewhere outside the Earth. That's where "The Martian Way" came in. Asimov's Martians went to Saturn to harvest ice from the rings, because they weren't getting enough water from Earth. *That's what we need!* I thought. Well, yeah, except that Asimov wrote that before we learned that the chunks of ice in the rings are way smaller than anything useful.

On the other hand, he also wrote it before we learned much about the Kuiper Belt. That was where the ice cubes I needed were hanging out; just a little farther out than Saturn. But we're living in the future, and I remember what Robert Heinlein said: LEO is half way to anywhere. Well, we can get to LEO, so we can get to the Kuiper Belt. At least, that's what I told my engineers. I didn't know how to interpret their expressions, but they knew how to interpret my "request": I was paying the bills, so they said "yes, sir."

But you can't just go grab an ice cube and throw it into the liquid of Earth's atmosphere. It'd be like dropping an ice cube into a glass of water: the water will splash out, and if the ice cube starts out high enough, it might even break the glass. You have to put it in gently. Actually, ideally, you put the ice cube in the glass, and then you pour in the liquid. For a little while, I thought about that, but then realized there was no way to take off the Earth's atmosphere to put the ice at the bottom, so I threw out that idea.

No, we had to find a way to gently put the ice cubes in. And then I remembered Doug Beason's "To Bring Down the Steel." He was talking about metallic asteroids: hollow one out, seal it in the vacuum of space, and its density would be low enough that it should just float in the air, like a balloon. Why not try that with an ice cube, I reasoned. And if it started to melt, well, it would just be rain falling on the ground, not Beason's tons of iron and steel.

So that's what we did: design propulsion units to bring icy comets in from the Kuiper Belt to near Earth orbit, design smaller vehicles to get those propulsion units out to the Belt, come up with a way of hollowing out the icy comets and sealing them over so they had vacuum-filled centers, and then lower them gently into the atmosphere, to cool things down.

As an aside, do you like how I say "we"? It was my money, but my engineering staff did the hard work (other than the hard work of actually accumulating all that money first).

At any rate, it was a brilliant concept.

All except the part about those floating ice balls cooling down the atmosphere, reversing global warming. Yeah, that didn't work, not one bit. Because—of course, you already knew—what my chemistry teacher said was the atmosphere can be considered fluid for certain calculations. Not liquid, fluid. Like I said, one false memory.

But the infrastructure we had to design, to bring in those inter-planetary ice cubes? That was what we used to build ourselves a space-faring civilization, to get people off this slowly over-heating rock ball and into the heavens.

And no, I'm not even going to talk about the false calculations that would enable any significant fraction of the population to get off the surface of Earth and into space. That's a whole other mistake of mine.

Bulkheads Make the Best Neighbors

(first published in *Analog Science Fiction and Fact*,
January/February 2020)

When I left Analog *to start* Artemis Magazine, *it was as part of a larger project—the Artemis Project—to design, fund, and build a colony on the Moon. (This was long before NASA realized "Artemis" was the appropriate name for the next Moon mission. Check out www.MoonSociety.org for more information on the project.) Though we didn't get there, the Moon and near-Earth space have been very important to me ever since. I'm also a big fan of Robert A. Heinlein's novel* The Moon is a Harsh Mistress *(even though it is now incredibly dated).*

There was also a bit of unplanned excitement, for me, about this story: it was published in the 90th anniversary issue of Analog, *for which there was a nice celebration. Hmm, that reminds me, I'd better start planning something for the centennial issue….*

"The groundhogs are acting up again—demanding 'recognition of the authority of the government' and expecting us to 'submit petitions for any large engineering projects to a review board.' They're a damn nuisance. Like any paper-pushing bureaucrat dirtside is gonna know the difference between a meteorite and a nickel-iron asteroid—"

"You got that right, Jimmy!"

"So what're we gonna do about it?"

"Fight! They don't know nuthin' 'bout nuthin' 'cept dirt. Let's show 'em who's boss!"

"Yeah, fine, but how we gonna show 'em, Dirk? This is a Hab Council session. We gonna call 'em names? Tell 'em we're independent? They may be sittin' at the bottom of the well, but they still got the big ships, an' the weapons."

"True, true. What we gotta do is get bigger weapons. Make 'em see the error of their ways. Show 'em we mean business, and they'll leave us alone."

"Yeah? And how long's it gonna take us to build a nuke bigger 'n what they got?"

"Forget bigger, Jimmy. Don't matter how big it is. If'n it c'n blow apart a hab, it's plenty big. No matter how big we c'n build 'em, ain't no way we're gonna blow apart their hab."

"Aw, c'mon, Maggie. Their hab's that whole big blue and green ball down there."

"My point, pr'cisely. Ain't no way we c'n outgun 'em, so we gotta outthink 'em."

"You got an idea, maybe?"

"Maybe. Somethin' you said… 'bout a groundhog bureaucrat not knowin' the diff 'tween a meteorite and an asteroid."

"It was this memo they sent. From the Department of the Interior. Warnin' us to make sure the new asteroid we're bringin' in don't get loose and smash down. 'Cept the bureaucrat kept callin' it a meteorite."

"That's it."

"What? Maggie, we cain't go droppin' no asteroid on 'em. Even if the government is a bunch of jerks, there's lots of people livin' down there's okay. We don' wanna kill 'em, jes' keep 'em out o' our hair."

"Well, then, that's it. We gotta build us a bulkhead. A bulkhead that'll keep them on their side, an' us on our side."

"I don' rightly follow you, Maggie."

"It's simple, Dirk. 'Member last week's memo? 'Make sure any and all debris created during EVA is retrieved and properly disposed of.' They don' want their precious ships smashing themselves on our junk, 'cause they cain't handle it. All we gotta do is put up a wall of junk, and they won't be able to get to us. Then we c'n let 'em yap all they want. Hell, we c'n even turn off the receiver. Won't matter to us what they want, when they're stuck down there."

"You may have somthin', Maggie. We c'n boost all the habs into higher orbits, and then fill the lower orbits with a whole lotta asteroids."

"You're close, Jimmy, but movin' a whole lotta asteroids is gonna take a whole lotta time. There's an easier way. All we gotta do is get a few decent asteroids into orbit, chop 'em up a bit to make a lot of pieces, and then start smashin' the pieces into each other. The 'debris' don't have to be big, but there's gotta be a lot."

"But it'll all decay, eventually."

"So? How long you think it'll take for an entire orbit's worth o' debris to decay, Dirk? And how long you think it'll take for us t' smash another asteroid or two to replace it? What're you scribblin', Jimmy?"

"Maggie, you're a genius. This'll keep the groundhogs down where they belong, an', after we get it set up, we'll only need another asteroid 'bout every year to keep up the bulkhead. Boy are they gonna be pissed when we tell 'em what we're doin'."

"We cain't tell 'em. Not 'til it's all set."

"Well, we got another asteroid due in in a month, and the next one after that'll be here in four months."

"That's it, then. We gotta start minin' the new one like always, but slow. Don't let on, and we gotta nice-nice the groundhogs 'til number two gets here. Then we start choppin' and smashin', and when number three gets here, we c'n jes' mix it in."

"Maggie, when we declare our independence in four months, I'm nominatin' you for President of the Habs."

"Only so long as I git to appoint you Ambassador to Earth."

Godding About and Sleeping Around:
Zeus' Conversation with Tantalus
(first published in the anthology
TV Gods: Summer Programming)

Editor Jeff Young told me the concept behind the anthology: "Take a television series, combine it with a mythology, and tell that story."

When How I Met Your Mother *debuted on television, I watched the first two episodes, and then gave up; it seemed like it was going to take too long to get to the point for me. But when I heard the series was ending, I watched the final episode. And then I read a little about it, realized that the whole series had been one grand experiment in non-linear story-telling, and got hooked on it. I watched the entire series in reruns (this was before on-demand bingeing was a thing). So when Jeff asked me for a story, I knew this was the series to emulate.*

"Son, I'm going to tell you an incredible story: the story of how I met your mother."
"But I'm already being punished."
"I know, but this is your break, so you can just sit there and listen."
"Uh, Dad, you caught me on the way to the kitchen. Can I grab a sandwich and get back to you?"
"Hang on, this'll just take a moment...."

I was soaring over the Saronic gulf when this cute little goat-nymph caught my eye. I just knew she was the one, but couldn't think of a way to separate her from the crowd of nymphs all around her. You know how those nymphs like to move in packs.

Anyway, I perched on a hilltop overlooking the meadow of the nymphs. I perched and I pondered, and then I saw a fast-moving shadow as an eagle flew by. Ah, inspiration comes from the strangest of places, doesn't it, son?

So I turned myself into a giant eagle, swooped down upon the nymphs, and managed to grab the object of my affections.

I carried her away, across the waters, to Oenone. After placing her gently on a bed of leaves, I transformed back into my more godly appearance, wooed the young lass, and had my way with her. Although I have to say, she had her way with me just as much. Let me tell you, son, those goat-nymphs really do know how to act like animals.

At any rate, when we had finished with each other, I gave her dominion of this island (which, I later learned, was eventually renamed for her), and some time later, she gave birth to… your half-brother Aeacus.

In the fullness of time, Aeacus grew to manhood, and then to become king of what was then known as Aegina (after his mother). Well, you know what a bitch your step-mother can be. Hera was pissed at Aeacus, and sent a dragon which carried off almost all the island's population. Really nasty dragon, that was.

So Aeacus, he was a king without a kingdom, and pleaded with me to restore his realm. Well of course I wasn't going to restore them: they were covered with dragon saliva, which is just… yuck. Instead, I managed to restore the population by turning the ants on the island into men. Aeacus again had his kingdom, Hera had her vengeance (for the moment), and the ants became the Myrmidons.

"But now that I come to think of it, the Myrmidons were there because of an earlier liaison of mine. Gee, I'm always planning ahead, even when I'm not doing it consciously."

"You planned to have an ant colony on the island?"

"Well, not precisely. You see, there was Eurymedousa. And some chicks are turned on by the strangest things..."

Fetishes are almost without logic. Some people are turned on by feathers, some by the whole chicken. For some, it's a specific material, or position, or location. It's beyond reasoning, and not worth trying to figure out.

But for whatever reason, Eurymedousa was incredibly turned on by... ants.

You know, if you want someone badly enough, you can go along with whatever they want, at least for a little while. I wanted Eurymedousa, so I turned myself into an ant.

To this day, I can't figure out why it worked with her, but it surely did.

We had a son, Myrmidon, who married, as most boys do, and had children, who had children... but somewhere down the line—either it was her kink or my transformation—but Myrmidon's descendants eventually turned into a colony of ants. And so it was, that when Hera's dragon carried off Aeacus's kingdom, the Myrmidons were there for me to turn them back into people, to repopulate Aeacus's realm.

* * *

"That's really interesting, Dad. Ants, no picnic, I get it. I'm just going to slip out and grab a bite…"

"Wait, just a sec. Did I ever tell you about Alcmene? You'll get a kick out of this. Alcmene as stunning: tall, gorgeous, brilliant… She had wisdom surpassed by no person born of mortal parents. Her face and dark eyes were as charming as Aphrodite's. And when she married, she honored her husband like no woman before her.

"But before that, I met her…"

Alcmene traveled with her betrothed, Amphitryon, to Thebes. He was on the road to redemption, and she was on the road to marriage. She wouldn't marry him until he had avenged the death of her brothers.

As they walked, they met a "beggar." "Stand aside, old fellow," said Amphitryon.

The beggar turned, and all but ignored Amphitryon as he ogled Alcmene.

"Mind your manners, grandfather," said Amphitryon, not unkindly, but sternly. He knew what Alcmene looked like.

The beggar, however, reached out and touched Amphitryon's arm, while staring at Alcmene. "She is marvelous," he mumbled. Then he turned away before Amphitryon could reach into his change purse.

The young couple passed out of sight over a rise, and I shook off the beggar image I'd been wearing. "I will have her," I said to myself.

Later, while Amphitryon was on his expedition against the Taphians and Teleboans, I visited Alcmene. But as the master of disguise, I was wearing Amphitryon's form.

"My beloved!" she greeted me at the door.

"I have returned. I have vanquished the Teleboans, destroyed the Taphians, and thought only of you." You know, as opening lines go, that's not too bad.

So I stayed with her for three nights, and then left. That night, the real Amphitryon returned, but Alcmene was already impregnated.

Several months later, I announced to all the other gods that a child would be born this day, a child of mine, who would rule them all.

Hera, once again showing her temper, prevented Alcmene's delivery, causing her great pain, and instead induced Nicippe to give birth (two months early) to Eurystheus. Alcmene later gave birth to Heracles, who grew to be one of the greatest Greek heroes.

"Sure, sure, I know all that, Dad. What's your point? And I'm getting hungry, you know."

"Just a moment, just a moment. What you don't know about that story is that Alcmene was one of my great-granddaughters, making Heracles my son and my great-great-grandson."

"Dad, you know, some of your relations—okay, a lot of your relations—are a little bit outre. Now, can we go to dinner?"

"Hang on. I haven't told you about satyrs. Do you know about satyrs?"

"Of course I know about satyrs, Dad. Everyone knows about satyrs."

"Yeah, well, but no. Everyone thinks they know about satyrs: goat-men, flutes, lust, but to really know about satyrs, you have to be a satyr. And once, I was."

"You were a satyr?"

"Let me tell you..."

* * *

It was Antiope. She was in a garden, looking as wantonly innocent as you can imagine. If she'd been frolicking with woodland creatures in a Disney movie, she wouldn't have looked out of place. Well, except that this is before Disney, and nymphs frolicking in the woods were usually unclothed. And as I later learned, it was just an image for her.

Anyway, I looked at her, and I felt... well, I felt like a randy satyr must feel.

Rather than spooking her by just appearing in the garden, I transformed myself into a satyr, and then emerged from the trees. And that was apparently the right move, because she wasn't shocked, wasn't scared, didn't bother trying to cover up. She looked at me, let her eyes wander half-way down my body, saw my desire, and came to me.

Let me tell you, those satyrs really have a way with themselves. I can't figure out why they call those little pills viagra, rather than just "satyr in a bottle." It was hot!

She was almost insatiable. Almost. But eventually, we sated each other, and when she fell asleep, I limped out of the garden. She was a handful, let me tell you.

So anyway, after I left her, Epopeus kidnapped her. But she didn't scream, she didn't fight. No, not Antiope. She took up with Epopeus where she'd left off with me. Man, what a hussy, even with that innocent-looking face.

So, comes the time, Antiope gave birth... to twins: Amphion and Zethus. But it turns out only one of them was my son: Amphion. Zethus was Epopeus' son. What a mess. Well, fortunately, the twin-half-brothers got along with each other. But as you might imagine, she wasn't much of a mother herself, and left the boys to be raised by herdsmen. Eventually, after the boys were grown, they reunited with their mother, and got along. Amphion, my son, became a great singer and musician. Hermes—you know Hermes, right? always trying to curry favor with me?—anyway, he gave Amphion a golden lyre, and taught him to sing. Zethus took after the men who had raised him, and became a hunter and herdsman. So yeah, you wouldn't think they'd get along, but sometimes opposites do attract, and the boys got on fine. Heck, they even got together to build the wall that fortified Thebes.

"So, a satyr?"

"Trust me, son. Would I lie to you?"

"Let's not go down that road, Dad. But satyrs are known for their appetites, right?"

"Well, yes…"

"Then let me tell you, my appetite is not being satisfied by this—"

"Unsatisfied appetite? Oh, that reminds me. You know Himeros, right?"

"Himeros?"

"Himeros, one of Aphrodite's kids, one of the Erotes."

"Um, yeah, I think we've met. Listen, I need a drink or something to nosh on. Can we pick this up later?"

"What? No. I'm telling a story here, c'mon, you'll like this one, I promise. Just cool your jets."

"So, Himeros?"

"Yeah, Himeros, the Erotes for sexual desire and unrequited love."

"Based on what you've been telling me, unrequited doesn't seem to be in your vocabulary."

"Very funny, son. But I'm just using him as a metaphor. See, the Arcadian king, Lycaon, had a daughter, and she was hot—"

"Did you ever met a woman who wasn't?"

"Hmm... not that I can recall. But anyway, Lycaon's daughter. She... well, I looked at her, and she was like sex on a pair of legs; just oozing desire and desirability."

"But there was a problem."

"Of course there was a problem. If she was just ready and willing, it wouldn't be much of a story."

"The way you brag, Dad, it would be right in your wheelhouse."

"Very funny. But not this girl. No, she became a nymph of Artemis; took the vow of virginity and everything. Let me tell you, a girl like this, it was just a waste."

"But you weren't going to let that stop you."

"Ah, how well you know me, my boy. No, of course I wasn't going let an ill-considered vow stop her from experiencing the fullness of life."

"How noble of you."

"Right. Well..."

She was in this glen, probably praying to Artemis because, well, what else was there for her to be doing? So I figured it was my golden opportunity. I disguised myself as Artemis, and walked out from behind a tree.

I actually had to rustle the branches a few times and clear my throat before she looked up from her praying. Then her eyes got big.

"Goddess! I... I didn't expect... why... how..."

Not real fast with the words, but with a body like that, I wasn't really there for conversation.

"I heard you, my daughter. You may be my most devoted follower, and I just had to meet you in person."

"I'm… honored… not worthy, my goddess. How may I serve you better?"

"You are already a paragon, dear Callisto. I've only come to enjoy your company, to bask in your attention."

Flattery, let me tell you, son, will get you almost everywhere. And Callisto, she was a sucker for it. It took me, literally, a minute and a half to get her naked and on her back. If she'd been one of those modern monotheists, you'd have thought she was experiencing the rapture. I mean, she was hot, but completely inexperienced, so it wasn't quite the rapturous experience I was hoping for.

Anyway, I knew she wasn't leaving the sisterhood for greater carnal knowledge, so I left her dozing after the experience. But several months later, she was bathing with several other nymphs when Artemis herself actually did show up. And while Callisto was inexperienced, Artemis knew exactly what she was looking at: Callisto was pregnant.

Well, Artemis flipped out. Absolutely insane. Bam, boom, she changed Callisto into a bear, and then bear-Callisto gave birth to Arcas.

She ran off, he grew up, and then years later, bear-Callisto came back looking for her son. He of course didn't recognize her as anything but a bear, and went out to kill her.

I know, I know, they call me love-'em-and-leave-'em Zeus, but I try to take care of my own. I couldn't let Arcas kill Callisto, so I put them up in the heavens, as the Great Bear and the Little Bear. See? There they are now.

* * *

"And what's your point here? That it's cool to be a lusty god if sometimes you're going to fake it as a lesbian?"

"Well, no... Not quite. Um. Where was I?"

"You were telling me about this 'forbidden fruit,' Callisto."

"Right. Well, the mortals call it forbidden fruit. As Zeus, you know, nothing is 'forbidden' to me."

"Dad, at this point, the only part of that phrase that interests me is the 'fruit,' part."

"Oh, yeah, forbidden. Well, Elara was another mortal I fell in love with."

"Dad, I think you need another term for it. You can't have 'fallen in love' with absolutely every female you ever ran into."

"I am a god, boy, and gods have big desires and great capacity. Stop interrupting."

"Sorry, sorry. So, Elara..."

"I met this mortal princess, Elara, and fell in love with her. It was a big love, very large, and I knew her, and she became great with child. Really great. It was a big baby. But I knew Hera would be pissed if she found out, so I hid Elara in a deep cave. And it was in that cave that she gave birth to Tityos. Unfortunately for Elara, Tityos was a giant, and... well... Elara died in childbirth. Let's leave it at that."

"Yeah, you seem really broken up over it."

"Well let me tell you about Tityos, and then you can decide how broken up I should be..."

Tityos emerged from the Earth, and some said he was the son of Gaia because that's where he came from. Unfortunately, I knew better.

Even more unfortunately, Hera found out. She got hold of Tityos, and talked him into raping Leto. Yeah, couldn't send her after poor Elara, so she decided to punish another of my women. Have I mentioned Leto yet? No? Well, I'll get to her. But for now, suffice it to say that she wasn't mortal; daughter of Titans, with her I begat Apollo and Artemis.

Anyway, Hera was livid, and sent Tityos on this mission of terror.

Tityos was out, stalking poor Leto, and he nearly had her, but fortunately for her, I had visited Leto earlier, and our kids, Apollo and Artemis, they were on the case. Artemis whisked Leto away while Apollo kept Tityos busy, and then they teamed up, and somehow (they've never actually told me how they did it), A and A managed to kill poor Tityos.

Yes, poor Tityos. Sure, he wasn't very nice, but he was my son.

Anyway, Tityos died, but you know this realm. You know death isn't necessarily the end.

The judges of the underworld, my sons Minos, Rhadamanthus, and Sarpedon, judged poor Tityos, and sentenced him. It's a bloody sentence, even makes me a little squeamish... they sentenced him to be bound to a rock in Tartarus. But that's not the bad part. The bad part is, they sent two vultures to feed on his liver. And then, his liver grows back each night. And each day, back come the damned vultures.

It's... well, it's not pleasant.

"Minos, Rhadamanthus, and Sarpedon? I don't think you ever told me about them."

"I haven't? Oh, well, that's a story you're going to want to hear. They were brothers."

"Full brothers? So far, it seems you haven't had more than one child with any woman, well, except you mentioned Apollo and Artemis—"

"I'm getting to them. But no, Minos, Rhadamanthus, and Sarpedon were full brothers. All three sons of Europa. But before I tell you about them, I have to tell you that—lies to the contrary—I never actually mated with Laodamia."

"You have to tell me that there's a woman you didn't have sex with?"

"Truth is truth, boy. I admit I got around, but not all the way around. Anyway, Laodamia. She was married to Evander, who was Sarpedon's son. But somehow a story came about that I had my way with her. But that would have meant I was sleeping with my son's daughter-in-law, and I just didn't do it. But I think I've finally figured out where the story came from: Sarpedon, my son, had an extraordinarily long life. Actually, he lived three life spans—a little gift from me. So when he showed up fighting in the Trojan War, the story-tellers assumed it couldn't possibly be my son Sarpedon, that he had to be someone younger. Then they concocted this scurrilous rumor that he was my second son Sarpedon. But that just wasn't true. Sarpedon did not have a grandson named Sarpedon, I did not have a second son named Sarpedon—that would be ridiculous, giving two kids the same name—and the exploits of both Sarpedons were all accomplished by one and the same man."

"Okay, I get it. You didn't seduce Laodamia."

"Right. But I was going to tell you about Sarpedon's mother, Europa. Man, was she a babe..."

Europa was Phoenician, daughter of King Tyre and Queen Telephassa, sister of Cadmus and Cilix.

She was the daughter of a king, and gorgeous, but kings in those days, well, they weren't always living in Buckingham Palace. Tyre had to make ends meet in more pedestrian ways. He had herds of cows, and I realized that was my way in with his daughter.

I transformed myself into a white bull, and mixed in with the herd while Europa was out tending them. I know I cut a fine figure as a god, but I'm not bad as a bull, for all of that.

I caught her eye, enticed her a little closer, and soon she was caressing my flanks. Even as a bull, let me tell you, it felt pretty darn good.

Eventually, she was enchanted, and climbed up onto my back. And that was the break I was waiting for. Ran with her down to the sea, I did, and started swimming.

She freaked a little, at first, but soon calmed down, realized she wasn't going in the drink as long as she held onto my horns, and I swam her over to Crete. Climbed up out of the water, and she slid down to the grass, so, right in front of her eyes, I transformed back into this female-seducing form. Apparently, it worked. She wasn't the least bit frightened, but started batting her eyelashes at me, and she had me naked almost before I knew what was happening.

She may have been playing the innocent maiden at home, but here on Crete, with no one around, she let loose her inner slut, and nearly exhausted me.

I wound up staying with her for quite a while. Well, for three sons, anyway.

Of course, I couldn't stay forever. I had godding work to get back to. But Europa, she wasn't going back to Phoenicia. She had three new sons, and a new island, so I made her the first queen of Crete.

But I didn't leave her empty-handed. I gave her three parting gifts: Talos, the bronze bull that guarded her, protecting her from pirates and invaders; Laelaps, the dog who never failed to catch what she was hunting (after all, Europa was going to need some help feeding our three kids); and a javelin that never missed, just in case Talos or Laelaps did.

After I left, she married Asterion, and he helped raise the boys.

Minos, the eldest, became the first king of Crete.

Rhadamanthus, the second boy, was actually more popular than Minos. And while they were ruling as co-kings, Minos got jealous, and forced Rhadamanthus out of the kingship, and out of Crete. He settled in Boeotia.

Sarpedon, Minos had forced him out even earlier, because they were both really interested in Atymnius, Cassiopeia's boy by Phoenix. He settled in Lycia.

The irony of Minos exiling his brothers is that, after they all died, they became the judges of the underworld, working together. I think—think—they've resolved their differences enough to work together.

"Come to think of it, Europa was a descendant of mine, too. Great-great-granddaughter, I think, from my liaison with Io: Io's son Epaphus; his daughter, Libya; her son by Poseidon—that randy, water-logged... anyway—Agenor was Europa's father. Hmm, well, I guess that's an example of a bonding with a descendant that worked out well. Anyway, I'll tell you about Europa later.

"But usually, mating with a descendant, there are problems. Have I told you about Danae, who was my g-g-g-g-g-great-granddaughter?"

"You're stuttering."

"You want me to spell it out? Fine. Danae was my great-great-great-great-great-great-granddaughter. That's six greats. Upon Io, I sired Epaphus, whose daughter, Libya, mated with Poseidon. Their son, Belus, fathered Danaus, whose daughter Hypermnestra's son Abas sired Acrisius, who was King of Argos, and the father of Danae..."

Acrisius wanted a male heir. Heck, don't all kings want male heirs? Well, he was pretty unhappy. But he was man enough to not blame Eurydice, his queen.

Acrisius consulted the oracle of Delphi, and the oracle, in a rare fit of clarity, told him he wouldn't have a son. But, she said, his daughter would indeed have a son. Acrisius felt some relief at that, but the oracle kept speaking: "That son will one day kill you."

"Shit," said Acrisius. Well, with that kind of prophecy, you can pretty well understand his disappointment.

But Acrisius wasn't a bad man. He wasn't about to kill off his only, beloved daughter Danae. Instead, Acrisius had a tall brass tower built, and installed in it a gorgeous room, draped in silks and fancy woods and precious gems... but with no windows and no doors. He sealed Danae in that room, walling it up. But he wasn't completely cruel, so he had a skylight built into the room, to let in light and air.

Well, I wanted Danae. I figured six greats was enough generations between us that the relationship wouldn't matter, and she wasn't really in a position to be picky, being walled up in a gorgeous, but inescapable, tower.

So I went to her as a golden rain, streaming down through the skylight on a cloudless day, and entered her womb, and soon after, our son, Perseus, was born.

Danae was… I guess surprised is a pretty good word for it. But that was nothing compared to Acrisius; he about flipped out. Here he'd gone to the trouble of building an impregnable tower—get it? That's a double-entendre, son—rather than killing his daughter, who was fated to bear the grandson that would kill him. And then she goes and has that child anyway. At that point, Acrisius was starting to get the message that there wasn't much he could do. But that didn't mean he was just going to roll over and die.

So he broke open the tower, hugged his daughter goodbye, and put Danae and Perseus in a wooden chest and set them adrift on the sea.

How he figured this was better than killing her outright, I'm not really sure. But Poseidon saw them on the sea—and he's a good guy—so he calmed it, kept the waves down to a minimum, and gave them a little current. They washed up on the shore of Seriphos, where the king's brother, Dictys, took them in, and helped raise Perseus.

Dictys's brother, King Polydectes, fell for Danae, and who could blame him? Heck, she was hot enough to attract me, and with that little bit of me running through her veins, well…

So Polydectes wanted Danae, but she wasn't interested. He was a king, so he felt he could make some demands. So he made a deal with her. He agreed not to marry her, but only if Perseus would bring him the head of the Gorgon Medusa.

You know how this part goes, I'm sure. Perseus was my seven-greats grandson, and also my son, so he could ask for some favor, and he got what he needed. He borrowed Athena's shield, Hermes's winged sandals, and

Hades's helmet of invisibility, and managed to do in Medusa.

On the way back to Seriphos, Perseus decided to have some more adventure, and stopped off in the kingdom of Aethiopia—no, not Ethiopia, the other one. In Aethiopia, Cepheus ruled as king with his queen, Cassiopeia. I'm sure I've told you about Cassi, she was a bit of a braggart. She had a pretty daughter, Andromeda, but claimed Andromeda was "equal in beauty to the Nereids." Well, you know how protective Poseidon is of the Nereids. He was ticked off. So he sent Cetus, the sea serpent, to destroy Aethiopia.

The oracle of Ammon made a prediction. The oracle said that "no relief would be found until the king exposed his daughter Andromeda to the monster." So Cepheus did it: he stripped Andromeda naked, and chained her to a rock on the shore.

So, by the time Perseus showed up, Andromeda was getting a little pruney from all her time by the water, and the people of Aethiopia were freaking out.

Perseus—that boy has a bit of an ego, but he is pretty damn good—said, "I can save the day," and he managed to slay Cetus, and then set Andromeda free.

Perseus fell for Andromeda. And Andromeda had only one condition: "You can marry me, if you promise to take me away from this place. My parents are just friggin' nuts!"

He promised, she married him, and they left town before sunset.

They eventually made it back home to Seriphos, where he showed Polydectes the Gorgon's head (which was probably starting to smell a bit by this time), and Danae didn't have to marry him.

Perseus set out for Argos, figuring to pick up where his childhood had left off. And when word of his approach reached Acrisius, he remembered what his oracle had said, and booked out of town. Actually, he went into a very rapid voluntary exile in Thessaly.

Perseus returned to Argos, and as soon as he got there, heard that King Teutamides of Larissa was holding funeral games to honor his father. Perseus had slain the Gorgon, slain Cetus, he figured he was a world-class athlete, so he headed out to Larissa, and entered the discus throw, because it was something new and exciting to him.

But sometimes you just can't avoid prophecies. In the audience was his aged grandfather, Acrisius. And Perseus, well, he was a world-class athlete, credit where credit is due, but he'd never actually thrown a discus. So his throw was a pretty darn good one: went farther than anyone else's, but it was so far off course that it went into the stands, and… well, you can see where this is going. Hit Acrisius in the head, killed him instantly, the poor old guy.

"So what's your point?"

"Well, it was 'better to avoid your descendants,' but now that I think about it, that whole being walled up in the tower put me in mind of Rapunzel, except the Grimms hadn't yet borrowed Friedrich Schulz's 1790 story, because Mademoiselle de La Force hadn't yet written 'Persinette,' because this was before Giambattista Basile had first written 'Petrosinella,' which was going to inspire her."

"What?!"

"What 'what?' The literary history, or the anachronism? I'm a god, remember? Let it go."

"I get it. You were all over the map back then. Are you done? Can I get you a drink while I get myself one?"

"But wait a moment, son, I was going to tell you about Io."

"Hey, you mentioned her before."

"I told you I'd get to her. I'm not just telling stories off the top of my head, you know."

"Sometimes, Dad..."

"Yeah, yeah, but in this case, the never-ending tale was how long it took me to hook up with Io..."

Io was the daughter of Melia, a nymph, and Inachus, the first king of Argos. In fact, she was one of Hera's priestesses in Argos...

Yes, you can see where this is going. What can I say? The heart wants what it wants, even though Hera would much rather have my heart hanging on her wall.

So, I noticed Io, and I wanted her. I knew Hera would throw a fit; she always gets upset when I go for another woman, and the fact that this particular one was already sworn to her would make it that much worse, but when I'm on the prowl, reason goes out the window.

So I made my move, and Io...

She turned me down. Cold. "I'm flattered, I'm honored, I would if I could, but no." Not "Maybe." Not "Let me think about it." Just a flat, one-hundred percent "No."

But you're not a god if you can take no for an answer.

I tried again. Again, I got nowhere.

Eventually, I took the problem to one of Argos's oracles. Fortunately, she wasn't bound to Hera, so I talked her into a plan. And yes, I know it was kind of devious, and not terribly nice, but hey...

So the oracle went to Inachus. Said she'd seen a sign, that Io had to go. And Inachus, well, you don't keep oracles around if you're not going to listen to them. Straight out the front door went Io, completely flabbergasted.

That's when I went to her again. Now she was on the run, I knew she wasn't ready for a quick roll in the hay; this was going to be the long game.

I offered to hide her from Hera. After all, kicked out of her father's home, she didn't have much of a future as a priestess. She agreed, somewhat reluctantly, so I turned her into a heifer. After all, I reasoned, if Hera was going to go looking for a missing priestess, she be checking two-legged beings, not furry four-leggers.

Yeah, well, you don't get to be Hera without having some wits. Hera saw right through the deception. But did she call me on it? No way. No, she can be just as sneaky as me, when she wants, which I guess is one of the reasons why I love her. So in this case, Hera begged me to give her the heifer that was Io as a present. Well, I couldn't say no, not without giving away the whole game, so I had to give heifer-Io to her.

But Hera kept up appearances; put heifer-Io in a lovely pasture, with soft sweet grasses, a lovely stream, trees for shade… and she set Argus Panoptes—the hundred-eyed giant—to watching heifer-Io, so I couldn't visit her.

It was maddening. Wheels within wheels; we both knew the other's game, and neither one of us could call the other on it. Heck, we couldn't even surrender. Just had to play on.

So there I was, wanting to un-heifer heifer-Io, free her, get her away, and do her. And there was Hera, keeping us apart, and making like she was enjoying having this pet heifer to take care of.

Eventually, I had to do something. The situation was untenable. So I talked to Hermes. He's fast, he's a storyteller. I figured he could help, and boy did he ever.

I was just hoping Hermes might be able to distract Argus enough that I could sneak heifer-Io out of the pasture, but Hermes went above and beyond. He told Argus stories, played his panpipes, and eventually, he lulled Argus into falling asleep.

Then, trickster that Hermes is, he slit Argus's throat. Killed him right in the pasture, under a tree where Hera wouldn't see; quiet and deadly.

I knocked down the fence, shooed heifer-Io, and she ran.

But Hera isn't long fooled. She saw heifer-Io running, and sent a gadly to sting her. And the gadfly kept stinging her. Driving across the world, so it seemed, never able to stop, never able to rest.

Eventually, she made her way across the Bosporus (although this was before it was named the Bosporus, in her honor), where she met Prometheus.

I think I told you about Prometheus, how I had to punish him for creating men, and for stealing fire to give to them. I chained him to a rock, where an eagle visited him every day to eat his liver. But Prometheus, like the other gods, is immortal, so his liver regenerates each night.

So Io met Prometheus, and he told her to take comfort from the knowledge that she would eventually be restored to human form, and that one of her descendants would become the greatest of heroes, Heracles.

Io continued on, escaping across the Ionian Sea into Egypt. And there, I met up with her, far from Hera's sight.

I transformed her back into human form, and we... well, you know what we did then.

Eventually, she gave birth to Epaphus, our son, and Keroessa, our daughter, whose son Byzas would go on to found Byzantium.

After I left Io in Egypt, she married King Telegonus. Their grandson, Danaos, eventually returned to Greece with his fifty daughters, who were known as the Danaids, and who will be immortalized in Aeschylus's play *The Suppliants*.

"Aeschylus? Wasn't he a couple of centuries later?"

"I keep telling you, son, I'm a god. Great capacities, infinite abilities, what do you think time means to me?"

"Fine, fine. You can see all of time at once. So can you see when you're going to be finished with this story so I can get something to eat?"

"None of your sass, boy."

"It's just that time is flying—"

"Flying, you say? I told you about the time I turned into an eagle, but did I tell you about flying around as a swan?"

"I have a feeling you're about to."

"Well, sure. You know Leda, right?"

"Leda? You mean Helen's mother?"

"Stepmother."

"Stepmother? That one I don't know."

"Then stop interrupting, and I'll tell you..."

Leda was a queen, married to King something-or-other... Tyndareus, of Sparta, that's it. She was one of the most fertile queens I ever met. Well, not exactly fertile. But eager... I guess if she'd been around in modern times, people'd have called her polyamorous. But back then, she was just really friendly, if you know what I mean.

So, Leda. It was like she had a big neon "Welcome" sign flashing over her bed chamber. I saw it one night, and decided to take her up on the offer.

Well, sometimes my timing is a little off. Turns out she'd just finished with her husband, who was snoring the loudness that comes of total satisfaction. But Leda, she was still up and about, wandering in the gardens.

I'm classy enough to know that some other guy wandering around wasn't going to get in there, so I transformed myself into a swan. You know, large, graceful, just the type of bird a girl would go for. Then I evoked an eagle, something to chase me, to get her sympathy going, and bang, there it was.

I fluttered down into the garden, this eagle chasing after me, and Leda, she scooped me up in her arms, petted me. "You poor thing," she cooed, chasing off the eagle. "You're so sweet. What a wonderful swan."

I was starting to get into this. The stroking felt good, her voice was all soft and loving, so I let my neck stretch a bit: long and sinuous, and snaking up her body, soft feathers stroking between her breasts...

It wasn't long before she got the hint, got a bit randy, and got goosed... so to speak.

Sometimes, my whims result in longer-lasting results than I'd intended. In the case of Leda, since I was a goose, she laid a couple of eggs. Not goose eggs, obviously, but people eggs. She didn't seem to think anything of it, and how she hid it from Tyndareus I'll never know. But one day, while she was dozing, I slipped another one in on her.

Nemesis and I had gotten together right about the time I'd been with Leda, but she wasn't interested in brooding a child-egg, so I took it and added it to Leda's clutch.

Then, right on cue, the eggs cracked, and out came the kids. For twins (well, quadruplets), the genetic mix-up was truly remarkable. There was Pollux, my son with Leda, Castor and Clytemnestra, her kids with Tyndareus, and Helen, my daughter with Nemesis.

So genetically, Castor and Clytemnestra were full siblings, twins. They shared a mother—and half their genetic complement—with Pollux. And Pollux and Helen were half-siblings through their shared father.

Fortunately for the kids, however, genetics hadn't been invented yet. Castor and Pollux grew up as twin brothers, knowing nothing else. And Tyndareus actually was a good guy; never showed that any of the kids might not be his, treated them all as beloved children, and they grew, as children will.

Later on, Leda and Tyndareus had a few more daughters—Timandra, Phoebe, Philonoe—all born in the more usual way: one at a time, viviparous births, and never a question about how the first four were born.

But Leda took to wearing feathers. All the time. Only feathers. Her silk gowns all went unworn; everything she wore was made of feathers. White feathers. Swan feathers. I guess she thought I was pretty good, eh?

"So you're saying any woman will fall victim to your charms, human or otherwise?"

"Well, not every woman, but I have to say my record is pretty good. And you know, I'm not the only one who gets around. I mean, other than not having the term, we

certainly had polyamory—don't roll your eyes at me; I'm telling you something."

"And telling me, and telling me... what you're not doing is letting me eat."

"Just listen, okay?"

Thyia was a naiad. She had a spring on Mount Parnassos, and her shrine was one of the first gathering sites for the Maenads. Well, except at the time, they were known as Thyiades... Thyades... whatever, the women who celebrated Dionysus with orgies.

Oh, speaking of which, I have to tell you about Dionysus and his mother. But I'll get to them.

Anyway, Thyia. She was a loving little naiad. Had a liaison with Apollo and bore him Delphos, for whom they named Delphi. She had an affair with Poseidon. And she was "close friends" with the nymph Chloris.

Actually, now that I think about it, she wasn't so much polyamorous as just a proponent of the Free Love movement of the '60s, except this was a couple millennia before the '60s.

Well, by the time she got around to me, she was slowing down a little bit. Actually, her bed-hopping had slowed so much that I was in hers for two sons: Magnes, who became the first king of Magnesia; and Makednos, whose descendants became the Macedonians.

"But I was talking about Leda, and you distracted me. The point of the story with Leda is that sometimes, hooking up with your own descendants brings a lot of disappointment."

"Didn't you already tell me about your liaisons with your offspring?"

"One or two of them, but there were others."

"What is it with you, Dad?"

"Hey, I'm not unique. It worked for Lazarus Long, didn't it? Although I think Bill Compton was kind of squicked by the concept. But I wasn't talking about twentieth-century literary characters; I was talking about me. So, Semele."

"Semele? Sounds familiar…"

"Semele, my great-great-great-granddaughter, from my son Epaphus and his daughter Libya—"

"You mentioned them before, didn't you?"

"Of course. I told you about her granddaughter Europa, and her four-greats granddaughter Danae. But now I'm telling you something else. My son Epaphus, his daughter Libya, her son Agenor, his son Cadmus, and then his daughter Semele, my four-greats-granddaughter. Semele was special to me…"

Semele was a priestess of mine. A good one.

One day, I watched her slaughter a bull on my altar—wow, could she wield a knife. The bull didn't feel a thing: one minute, alive; the next, an offering.

Well, you know about bulls: they're big, and when you slaughter them, there's a lot of blood. Semele was good, but there's not much you can do to avoid getting bull blood all over you when you slaughter one. So after the offering, she jumped in the river Asopus to clean off.

I was watching, because… well, the offering was nice, but Semele in the nude was even nicer. I watched, and I thought, "here's this priestess, and she can handle a knife, and she looks great, too.…" You know what comes next.

But this time, it wasn't just lust. I really fell for her. Of course we did it that afternoon, but afterward, I found myself thinking about her, and I had to go back to her, again and again.

It turned into a relationship, which is pretty rare, let me tell you.

Unfortunately, I went back a little too often, and Hera twigged to what was going on.

So she appeared to Semele as an old crone, a potential worshipper, and befriended her. Eventually, Semele broke down, and told Hera I was her lover. Hera—sometimes, she can be a real bitch, you know?—pretended not to believe her, kept asking her if she had proof that her lover was really Zeus, and like that.

So one day, when I'm with Semele, she tricks me. Asks me to do her a favor. "Anything," I said, because I had real feelings for her. "Whatever you ask, I shall grant."

So she says "prove to me you really are Zeus. Reveal yourself in all your glory."

You know what happens in cases like that. She was enough generations removed from my descent that she really was mortal, so I begged her to ask for something else. But no, she was insistent: "Prove yourself to me."

I tried. Oh, how I tried. I showed her the smallest possible lightning bolt I could manifest. I called the sparsest, weakest thunder cloud you can imagine. I tried to save her. But she was mortal, and mortals cannot look upon we gods without incinerating.

It was a horrible conflagration. Turned my stomach, not to mention breaking my heart.

But as she burned, I realized she was pregnant. Let me tell you, I was ready to incinerate Hera for that little trick.

But I grabbed the fetus, pulled it from the flaming Semele. It was too little, not ready to be born. What could

I do? I sewed it into my thigh, where baby Dionysus came to term, and was born, a few months later.

Of course, I had to avoid Hera for those months: she would have noticed the lump on my thigh. And when it was the baby's time to be born, I went away to the mountains, hid myself, and gave birth to the baby.

But you know me, you know I wasn't in any position to be this new baby's mother. So I called in Hermes to help with child-rearing.

From there, I'm not really sure how Dionysus grew up. Over the years, he and Hermes have given me several different stories: he was raised as a girl by King Athamas and Queen Ino; the rain-nymphs of Nysa brought him up; Rhea looked after him; Persephone brought him in the Underworld... I'm not really sure.

But I next met him after he'd grown up. He was going off to rescue his mother from Hades. After he brought her back to the overworld, I brought her up to Mount Olympus, set her up under a new name—Thyone—and now she presides over the frenzies Dionysus inspires. We don't see each other much, and Hera seems to have gotten over her pique, at least in that particular case.

"Which brings me to your mother. Oh, but look at the time. That's the end of your break. I'll tell you the rest some other time, but now, you have to go back to standing in your pool, Tantalus."

"..."

"And if you see Sisyphus on your way out, tell him I've got a story he needs to hear."

Mars is the Wrong Color
(first published in *Nature*, October 2, 2008)

I was very excited to sell this story, because it marked my first professional short fiction sale to a magazine other than Analog. *I was a professional author: the checks I cashed from* Analog *attested to that fact. But I felt like a one-trick pony. Thus, making a sale to another magazine—in this case, one that published only one piece of fiction per issue (*Nature *is a British science journal)—was a great boost to my self-esteem.*

And the fact that Nature *paid nearly twice as much as* Analog *(I think it was 12 cents per word, compared to* Analog*'s 5–8 cents) didn't hurt, either. (Yeah, nobody's getting rich writing short fiction.)*

There's a difference between a conspiracy and what Margaret Mead called "a small group of thoughtful, committed people." The former will always fail, because someone will give it away. The latter, as Mead said, "can change the world. Indeed, it is the only thing that ever has."

Many ventures fail not for a bad idea or poor planning, but because the wrong group of people are involved. I'd learned that time and again in my organizing efforts: fan groups, idealistic businesses, and even social organizations that sputtered along but eventually collapsed because the people involved didn't mesh well, or didn't have the right skill sets.

This time, I vowed, it would be different. This time, my goal dwarfed all the others, and required far more commitment and cohesion amongst the people I'd be gathering to carry out the plan. So I went slowly. I didn't start with public pronouncements or marketing campaigns or mass appeals to everyone I knew.

Instead, I slowly found people of like mind through quiet, one-on-one conversations. I found my potential collaborators at scientific conferences, through friends and business acquaintances, and, in one instance, a call out of the blue to an author who wrote something in a story that resonated with me.

It was a large group for a conspiracy, but a small number of people to carry out such a grandiose plan. And this one time, finally, I knew before I asked that they would all say yes. I convinced my double handful of potential co-conspirators to get together at a quiet resort during the off-season. They all said yes to the first date I proposed.

After the introductions were out of the way, I think they all realized I had something larger in mind than a social gathering. I stood up, and everyone else fell silent, looking at me with anticipation.

"Mars is the wrong color," I said. "After so many missions looking for life, I think we can be fairly certain that there is none on Mars. There may once have been, but there's nothing now, and the environment won't permit anything we'd recognize as life to grow."

There were nods of agreement around the room, and an encouraging, "Yes, go on."

"We can keep going as we have been, sending probes to Mars every two years to investigate smaller and smaller possibilities, or we can gather a small group of people," I looked around the room with purpose, and knew they were the right crowd, because every one of them met my eyes and smiled, "and admit there's no life, but that it's time to start seeding it.

"NASA is launching the Firebird in a year. It will be a successor to the Phoenix, with a soil laboratory, a digging arm, and mobility."

It was definitely the right crowd. I didn't have to finish the concept before someone else said, "The Flora experiment. We'll need to co-opt it, make it smaller and lighter than the program integrators expect."

"Then we can take the extra space and put what in it?"

"Extremophiles. Some sort of microbes that can tolerate the current Martian environment, which will excrete—"

"The oxygen and ozone we need to transform the environment."

"Someone will notice."

"By then, it'll be too late to stop the process. If word doesn't get out, the rest of the world may assume it's a natural process."

"Or a miracle."

"But we'll know better."

"We won't have a living Mars to visit, nor will our grandchildren."

"No, but their grandchildren will. Governments move too slowly, and don't think far enough ahead."

"Better a second habitable planet in a bunch of generations than none at all."

"If we're caught…"

"What? No country I know has a law against terraforming Mars."

"But they'll come up with something. Theft of government services? Deceit? Lying to a federal agency?"

"Then we'll pay a fine or go to jail."

"But Mars will live."

"What do we call the project?"

"If there's a name, there will be something to give us away. Something to let slip."

"Don't use your government e-mail accounts to talk about this with anyone."

We broke up into working groups. One to decide which microbes to send. Another to build their flight compartment. Yet another to redesign Flora to make room for our unannounced package. And those who would be inspecting the craft before launch, who were necessary to overlook our modifications. By the end of the weekend, we came back together, and we had a workable plan. The scheduling was going to be tight, but that only meant less time for our plot to be discovered and stopped.

We all left that weekend vowing to carry out our plan without telling a soul: not our spouses, not our children, and leave not a word in our wills. What we were doing, we were doing for all humanity.

I organized the group: that was my contribution. I'm not a scientist, not a biologist, I don't work for NASA, and I had nothing more to do with any of the project members. But ego is a funny thing. As the organizer, I feel a certain responsibility to them, to let the world know that there is hope; the hope of another planet for our grandchildren's grandchildren, if only we can keep ourselves alive long enough for Mars to be ready. Firebird will land on Mars very soon; there's nothing anyone can do now to stop the process, short of nuking Mars, but that's not going to happen. So I've written this story.

Keep looking up, and tell your children. There will come a time when Mars is no longer the red planet. Watch for the white clouds, the blue water, and the green life. It's coming.

It's the Thought that Counts
(first published in
Analog Science Fiction and Fact, April 1998)

*This was originally one of my recursive stories. It was
written specifically for* Analog, *and Stan bought it on the
first try (it may have been my last story submission while
I still worked for the magazine), but he decided to change*
Analog *to* Stupefying Stories *so he didn't get in trouble
with the publisher.*

"We're dead. Circulation is down again this
year—this is the lowest it's been in five years. If this
keeps happening, the publisher's gonna shut us down
for sure. How are we gonna get those numbers back
up?"

"Clone the readers?"

"Yeah, right. Get cell samples from each one, and
then implant them in available women, and wait fifteen
years for them to start reading the magazine? We'll be out
of business before then, if they don't jail us first."

"Well, we've always said that it takes a certain mind
set to read *Stupefying Stories*. What if we simply clone
that mind set?"

"Clone the mind set?"

"Yeah. The Human Genome Project is finished—we
know where all the genes are. Now all we need to do is
get a representative sample of readers, figure out which of
the gene patterns we want to select for, and then start
distributing them."

"How? Free diskettes?"

"Ha ha. No, seriously, we'll use genetic engineering. A retrovirus to modify a few genes should do it."

"Won't people notice, when they start wanting to read *Stupefying Stories* after never having read science fiction before?"

"Sure they would—if we distributed the retrovirus randomly among the population. But that would be bad. We need to target our audience to people who might have picked up *Stupefying Stories* already—push them along in the right direction. And then make sure *Stupefying Stories* is the first science fiction magazine they see. We should seed the retrovirus into schools, specifically, science classes, starting at like high school."

"Is that it? Create the retrovirus, spread it in high schools, and stand back?"

"Well of course not. Once we've prepared the minds to read *Stupefying Stories,* we have to give them the opportunity to learn that *Stupefying Stories* exists. If we can get one copy into the hands of a student we've prepared to want the magazine, we'll have a lifetime subscriber."

"And that means…?"

"That means we're gonna have to convince the publisher to spend some money on publicity and advertising."

"Like I said, we're dead. The publisher's gonna shut us down for sure."

The Necessary Enemy
(first published in the anthology *If We Had Known*)

After my sale of "Shall Not Perish from the Earth" (see earlier in this book), I realized that writing for anthologies could be a lot of fun. So when Mike McPhail told me about this anthology he was editing, and offered me a slot, I jumped at the chance. Unfortunately, the story I wrote was way too short (see "The Ant and the Grasshopper," later in this volume). Fortunately, there was enough time before the deadline for me to try again, and the result was this story.

Yang and yin, light and dark, good and evil. The philosophers have known all along. But seeing the applicability of philosophy to real life has never been humanity's strong suit.

If we had realized that it takes a villain to make a hero. If we had realized that we needed an enemy in order to be the victor. If we had realized a ruling party needs a loyal opposition....

"Make America Great Again" started off as a campaign slogan, and became a political rallying cry. But as with most political slogans, it was only half-right. Where the slogan failed was in ignoring the fact that, in order to be great, America had to be compared to something else, had to have an equally great enemy to contend against.

America's rise to greatness began with the Civil War. In those years of horror and death, the Northern states finally came together as a coherent whole, truly a united nation. After the war, it took a long time to integrate the Southern states into that whole.

When Theodore Roosevelt launched the Great White Fleet, he was announcing America's intention to take a major role on the world stage, and by the time of World War I, the USA was on its way to greatness. From the American point of view, the war was brief, giving Americans the impetus to build up to a war footing without the drain of actually fighting a terribly long war. And at war's end, the USA grabbed center stage as a powerful player. Even if the nation rejected Woodrow Wilson's League of Nations, his actions in Paris served notice that the United States was a major player. And then World War II truly brought America to the top of the heap.

But it wasn't simply domestic will that made America a superpower, it wasn't merely the creation of the atomic bomb. It was the fact that we faced enemies of equal stature. During that war, it was Nazi Germany and the Empire of Japan, both of whom were sent to ignominious defeat.

At the end of the war, the leaders of the free world foresaw the rise of the Soviet Union, and promulgated the Bretton Woods agreement to guarantee the peace of the free world. Maintaining that agreement, guaranteeing free passage of the seas, made the USA a superpower.

And the rise of the Soviet Union gave the United States a true adversary, an equal but opposite superpower against whom to contend. Thus, the USSR, more than anything else, is what made America great.

It was because of the USSR that the USA came together to put a man on the Moon. In 1962, John Kennedy spoke at Rice University, and while everyone remembers him saying "we will put a man on the Moon and safely return him to Earth during this decade," it was the reasons leading up to that statement that truly kicked the American space program in the ass. In the prefatory paragraphs of his speech, he said "for the eyes of the world now look into space, to the moon and to the planets beyond, and we have vowed that we shall not see it governed by a hostile flag of conquest, but by a banner of freedom and peace…. Whether it will become a force for good or ill depends on man, and only if the United States occupies a position of pre-eminence can we help decide whether this new ocean will be a sea of peace or a new terrifying theater of war…. Within these last 19 months at least 45 satellites have circled the earth. Some 40 of them were 'made in the United States of America' and they were far more sophisticated and supplied far more knowledge to the people of the world than those of the Soviet Union…. To be sure, we are behind, and will be behind for some time in manned flight. But we do not intend to stay behind, and in this decade, we shall make up and move ahead." It wasn't that the moon was a great place to go; it was that we had to beat the commies to get there. An adversary pushing, not a goal pulling.

And after we won the space race, it was because of the USSR that the USA built the largest, most powerful navy the world have ever known. It was because of the USSR that the USA strove to excel in the sciences, in economics, in pretty much every field of endeavor.

Unfortunately, we slipped up. We didn't think deeply enough about the conflict. We lost sight of our need for the Soviet Union's existence, and started thinking of them as an enemy to actually be defeated. Thus, Ronald Reagan's SDI program—perhaps accidentally—did force the USSR to spend itself into bankruptcy. It wasn't long after that the USSR fell apart, leaving the USA as the world's only superpower. And in the glory of that triumph, we didn't realize it heralded our own coming slide. But George Orwell had pegged that one, with the never-ending war in *1984*.

Without a proper enemy, maintaining our stature as a superpower became a nearly futile exercise. That status began to invite attacks, not by another superpower, but by gnats, mosquitos, tiny groups of feral dogs bent on taking down the biggest kid on the block. Not unlike an elephant, which is able to stomp a lion, but can be taken down by a pack of jackals, the United States was open to attack by tiny groups of religious zealots.

That's why, though we did (unfortunately) win the Cold War, we could never win the "War on Drugs," the "War on Poverty," the "wars" of terrorism, nor defeat any of the other invented, too-small enemies. We could never invent an enemy great enough. Consider *TNG*'s episode, "Elementary, Dear Data": a villain has to be able to win to make the fight worth fighting.

So we find ourselves in need of an enemy. A great enemy. One worthy of our stature.

And we can look beyond our own greatness. As we gathered a coalition of allies to win World War II (and tried to build coalitions for the later, tinier wars), we can once again gather a coalition of nations—if we can present them with a truly great, truly awesome enemy, one that requires our combined efforts.

We need an alien invasion. We don't want *Star Trek*'s Vulcans, lending a helping hand. The self-loathing of *Avatar* would do more to keep us at home. Even the mindless planet-killers of *Armageddon* or *Deep Impact* probably wouldn't serve to elicit our best efforts. What we truly need is *Independence Day*. We need a massive alien invasion that threatens to destroy all life on Earth. That… that would be an enemy awesome enough and mighty enough to make us once again great.

But you know, there's just never an alien invasion around when you need one.

That's why I called you, individually and specifically, here in secrecy within the relative anonymity of the International Space Development Conference. Within this room, I believe, are the minds that can convince the world of a coming alien threat. You were specifically chosen for your backgrounds. Among you we have scientists, engineers, fictioneers… people representing all the fields of human endeavor necessary to convince the public that we face an existential threat, and that we can overcome that threat.

I'll say it before you can: as scientists, we're dedicated to the search for truth. Are we abrogating that public trust if we lie an alien invasion into existence? Yes, in the short term, we probably are. But in the longer term? I think we've all said, at one time or another, that the greatest threat to humanity's survival is not leaving the surface of the planet. So if perpetrating the lie that an alien invasion is coming can be the driving force to get us to expand into space, do you think we could live with ourselves?

What do you say? Shall we get down to the business of lying to humanity?

That recording was made surreptitiously by my great-grandfather. And every day after that conference ended, he devoted himself to helping humanity prepare for the alien threat. For three generations, our family has worked in the great endeavor. But I still believe it was that gathering, that discussion, that was the sole driving force that got humanity off the surface of Earth in a meaningful way, that drove us to develop the orbitals, and Moonbase Artemis, and the *Traveler*. And now, as you're getting ready to join the first wave of humanity to voyage beyond the confines of the Solar System, it's time to pass the burden of knowledge on to you. Only you can decide when or if your fellow travelers will be ready to learn that their voyage is predicated on a myth. That there really is no imminent alien invasion. I leave it to you to decide when they will have reached the stage of saying "If we had known, we would have gone anyway."

Creatively Ignorant

(published in the anthology *Footprints in the Stars*)

This was for the sequel anthology to If We Had Known *(see the previous story). This time, I tried something a bit odd: because there is so much dialogue, and so much of it is a character relating a previous conversation, I tried writing it without quotation marks, but just introducing each scene. The editors weren't too happy with that, so I rewrote the story, including the quotation marks, but taking out the third-level conversations so that I didn't have any lines looking like "'"This conversation is going to be quoted by someone who will be quoted by another," Jim said,' John said."*

Never had I been so scared of someone who was so polite. Neat suit and tie, aviator sunglasses, impeccable haircut, and wired ear piece. He didn't have to show me a badge for me to know he was Government.

"I'm here about the coins," he said, after I opened the front door.

"What coins," I asked. I'm a writer, but not an ad-libber.

His expression told me he was Serious, and I'd better not screw around.

I stepped back, and he stepped in. Behind him, I saw another fellow dressed just like him, lurking in the shadows on the front porch. And at the curb, a Nondescript car was idling.

The coins. Like most writers I know, I have a wide variety of interests and hobbies. One of them is numismatics, but looking through my pocket change one day, I came across two coins I did not recognize.

I checked online, but couldn't find these coins anywhere: about the size of quarters, silvery color, but no reeding, and the lettering on them was nothing I'd ever seen before.

So I did what I always do when I find a coin I can't identify, or that I think might have some value: I put them aside until the next time I was going to be near Stacks, and then brought them in with me. The staff there are walking encyclopedias of numismatic knowledge, but they managed to surprise me: no one there could tell me anything about the two coins. They photographed them, to share with other dealers. Surely someone would know. Normally, if they can't identify a coin, they assume it's not a legal tender coin, but just a metal disc with some designs on it. But for some reason, they felt these might be something more. I left them my phone number, in case they turned up anything.

And then Mr. Government knocked on my door.

"Please bring the coins," he said.

And though I might have thought about taking decoys, I looked at him, and any pretense at subterfuge deserted me. I took the coins out of a drawer.

I locked the door on the way out, and when we got to the car, he said, "May I have your cell phone, please?"

Though it was phrased as a question, I knew there was only one answer he would accept, and handed it to him.

He said, "Thank you," and put the phone in a solid looking little box in the car. Lead-lined, I assumed.

He sat in the back with me, but his manner rejected all conversation. As we pulled away from the curb, I realized I couldn't see out the windows.

* * *

Some indeterminate time later, the car stopped, and we got out, in an enclosed, featureless garage. He escorted me—oh so cordially—down a bland hallway to a completely unmemorable room.

"Thank you," said the man sitting at the table. My escort nodded and left, closing the door.

Before I could even begin to ask inane questions, he said, "No, you're not under arrest. You're being held pending determination."

"What determination? Whose?"

"Actually, mine. Determination of… well, to explain your situation, let me tell you about mine first. You're a writer, as I once was, which is why I'm the one conducting this interview. But before we begin, may I please have those 'coins'?"

Looking around the bare room, I knew I didn't have a choice, and handed them over.

He nodded his thanks, stepped to the door, and handed them to someone outside. Then he sat back down. "My story," he said. "I wrote mostly science fiction, but I tried anything I thought could inspire others. No dystopias—they didn't entertain me, and I wanted to entertain my readers, to give them hope and inspiration.

"It wasn't a full-time career; just a paying hobby. I knew I wasn't going to make a living writing fiction, but when people asked what I did, writing was the only thing I mentioned. The other things, the day-jobs, were just to put food on the table and a roof over my head. But when I wrote fiction, that was when I was truly alive.

"And I came to it because that's how I'd grown up: reading and watching it. Reading those incredible word pictures of a future that could be, if only…. I actually started with television. *Star Trek* was the first, the one that made the greatest impression on me. I was so upset when I learned that *Star Trek* was just fiction, that I couldn't travel between planets like that. And yet… it didn't crush me. It was that vision of a future which could be that encouraged me. I began to read. Not only fiction, but science. I learned what we knew, what we could do, and what we'd need to learn to get there. It wasn't too many years before I realized I wasn't going to be the scientist who'd figure out how to get us there—as much as I wanted to be. But I also learned of the vast numbers of working scientists who claimed science fiction had encouraged them to go into the sciences, and that… that was something I could do.

"I started, as most writers do, crafting stories based solely in my imagination. Well, not solely. Some of them were based on my extensive reading. But they were purely imagination.

"Eventually, I got to the point where I wanted to add more verisimilitude to my stories, and I started doing actual research. I found that I enjoyed the research almost as much as the writing. At first, it was tracking down obscure facts. The internet is useful, but there are still undiscovered minutiae lurking in the physical world that haven't—won't—be translated into the electronic… as you discovered.

"I started in used book stores, looking for specific things I needed for specific stories. But over time, I branched out, became a lot less selective. As a writer, you never know what you're going to need or when, what's going to stimulate an idea. We writers are magpies. I bought books that looked interesting, books that looked well used, and sometimes just the book next to the one I was looking for, for the serendipity of it. Several times, I discovered things on my bookshelf with no idea about where they'd come from or why they'd interested me, but which turned out to be absolutely vital for the piece I was working on.

"That's why one day, as I flipped through a book from my shelf that I couldn't recall ever seeing before, I came across a strange inscription that I couldn't read. But there was something about it that made me think it was important. It wasn't the Voynich manuscript, but it was, as I later learned, a completely unknown language.

"After spending several hours pondering that inscription, I put it aside and finished the story. But that book moved from my stacks of 'someday I might need it,' to 'this is interesting, I'm going to hang on to it.'

"As frequently happens, I soon forgot all about that book. I moved on to other stories, other research, other puzzles. I kept writing, kept acquiring books and reference materials.

"Then I discovered the joy of travel, and of putting real people, real places, into my stories. Many people travel for vacation; writers travel for research.

"Once I found myself on a trip to… well, it doesn't matter where, because the land has since been secured. At any rate, I was walking through some fascinating caves, and found carving on a wall. Strange marks, definitely not a language I knew, and yet familiar. I took many photographs, from every angle. I'd originally planned to be there for a few hours; I wound up staying for a week, exploring the entire cave system.

"And when I got home, I realized why those markings had seemed familiar: they were the same as the strange language in that book.

"Well, in addition to being a writer, I like puzzles. And this, I decided, was a puzzle. What could the markings possibly mean? They had to make sense to someone, but they were so alien…

"I spent days puzzling over it, and eventually, sought help. I posted pictures on the web… well, I tried to post pictures. But the system failed each time I clicked 'post.'

"I figured I was tired, doing something wrong, and I'd try again the next day. But the next day came, and I again tried to post them, and the same thing happened.

"I posted other pictures of my trip, no problem. I tried the symbols again, and nothing doing.

"Sometimes I'm a little slow on the uptake, but I do get there eventually. These specific pictures were being blocked. Therefore, there was something important about them.

"I puzzled over those symbols from the cave, and the symbols in the book, and eventually, they started to make some kind of sense to me. I could see repetitions, congruencies, and connections, but I just didn't have enough of them to translate. I had a hunch they were a language, so I dug out images of written languages.

"I couldn't find these symbols anywhere.

"I turned it into a methodical search, checking out every language we use on this planet. Still no joy.

"Then I went to dead and extinct languages. Of course I knew that no one speaks Latin anymore, that Aramaic, hieroglyphs, Cuneiform had eventually been deciphered. And they led me to Linear A, the Cypro-Minoan syllabary, and Isthmian: languages we still aren't able to understand.

"So I went back to haunting used book stores, looking for more of those symbols. But since serendipity had brought me to the first book, I knew a targeted search wasn't likely to bring results, and for a time, it seemed like I'd been right.

"Eventually, I decided there must be other people puzzling out the same mystery. Rather than trying to post my photographs, I drew a few pictures that were similar, but not identical, to the photos I'd taken and the book.

"And again, my posts wouldn't go through.

"This time, though, a chat window popped open on my computer. Odd, that, since I never used a chat feature. But there it was: a message about my unpostable pictures. 'Where did you see those symbols?'

"I decided to play along, typing, 'In a cave, and in a book.'

"'Where is the cave?'

"'Why should I tell you?'

"'That's a good question,' my anonymous messenger replied. 'We'll be in touch.'

"A few hours later, just after dinner, there was a knock on my front door, probably just like the knock you got this evening."

I grunted agreement. And he described a ride almost identical to the one I'd just taken.

"Eventually, we arrived... well... here. And I was escorted into... actually, I think it was this very room, and I had a conversation with Director Smith. He didn't give me a chance to get settled. 'I saw your pictures of that cave. We thought we'd found them all, but apparently not. If you'd be so good as to tell me where it is, we can secure it, as well.'

"'Just a minute,' I said. 'What's going on here?'

"'You'd like me to spell it all out for you? You were already puzzling it out yourself. But if you're the thinker we think you are, you don't need me to tell you.'

"'Well, obviously those markings really are some sort of language I don't recognize.'

"He nodded."

"'And since I've looked at a lot of them, I'm pretty sure it's not a terrestrial language.'

"His eyebrows rose.

"'But if you're so interested in it that you're able to block me from uploading pictures, you already know all about it, and have probably translated it all.'

"No real reaction.

"'And if you have already translated it, you'll let me go once I tell you where the cave is.'

"At this, he finally reacted. Just a slight downturn at the corners of his mouth, but I saw it.

"'I'm not leaving?'

"'That depends on how much you care about humanity, how much you can extrapolate.'

"'I get the feeling you want to tell me something,' I said.

"'Want? No. I'd be much happier if you'd tell me where that cave is, hand me the book, and then decide you hadn't seen anything at all. But we both know that's not going to happen.'

"'We're at an impasse, aren't we?'

"He frowned.

"At the time, I liked to think I was an intelligent, creative person. I could tell he felt trapped by circumstance, but that he was also serving a higher purpose, and me, my freedom, my very life, did not factor into his considerations.

"Suddenly, I knew, with absolute certainty, that I was here to plead for my life.

He came out of his reverie, and looked directly at me for the first time in his recitation. "Before I go any further, have I convinced you?"

"Convinced me of what?"

His mouth turned down, but he continued. "'I'm not a linguist,' I said to him, 'but I have to assume that, if that language could have been deciphered, it would have been. And if it was deciphered, I would have found a match somewhere. If it was completely undecipherable, you wouldn't care so much; it would be just another curiosity, like the Voynich manuscript. But since I'm here, I have to assume it's not just a curiosity.'

"'The only reason you would have to know who I am and bring me here is because that language does mean something more to you than just pictures.'

"'That means you have deciphered it. And if you have deciphered it, but it's completely unknown, that means you're keeping it a secret, and such a deep, dark secret that you don't even want me to talk about its existence.'

"He quirked an eyebrow, so I kept theorizing.

"'If it were an ancient language you've managed to decipher, what could it possibly say? "The tribe killed an animal, so we didn't starve"? Doubtful. If that's all it is, you wouldn't care.'

"'But you obviously care, so it's something more.'

"'I've written my share of secret history stories, but I know they're just fiction. So it's not just some ancient language. It's something more.'

"'The carvings I saw in that cave—'

"He interrupted me to note that I still hadn't told him where the cave was.

"This time, it was my turn to nod knowingly. 'My security,' I said. 'Once I tell you, you don't have any reason to keep me alive.'

"He nodded.

"'Those carvings weren't recent, not some secret code that's escaped your control. They have to be something old, really old.'

"'So… old, secret, don't want to share it with the world, not secret history… I'm talking myself into a conclusion I'm having a hard time believing.'

"'Remember Sherlock Holmes,' he said.

"'Have I really eliminated the impossible?' I asked.

"He nodded.

"'Then what does it say?' I asked.

"He sighed, and then became far more loquacious. 'Before I tell you what it says, I want you to tell me what it means.'

"I knew he wasn't just playing at words. He didn't mean the meaning of the inscriptions; he meant their very existence.

"I must have sat there for two minutes. Unmoving, unblinking, while my mind moved at warp speed."

Again, he focused on me. "So, do you know what I was thinking?"

As he must have done those years ago, I sat there, letting "nah, couldn't be" escape from my mental vocabulary. Eventually, I blinked my drying eyes.

"Fermi," I said.

"Go on."

"Fermi's Pardox, and the time variable in the Drake equation means that, though intelligent life may exist somewhere/somewhen in the time/space continuum, the odds of us meeting that life are exceedingly small. But that life did exist, and even visited."

He nodded.

"The carvings, the language you found—and the… coins… I found, the reason I'm here—are all really ancient, but more than that, their origin isn't terrestrial. Do you know how old?"

"On the order of 100,000 years."

"Right. But just proof of an alien language wouldn't be a cause for all this secrecy. You've actually translated it… And it says something much deeper than 'Joe was here.'"

"Keep going."

"In order to mean anything, there has to have been more than what you found in the cave."

"And in the book," he added meaningfully. "And the coins you found. Yes, much more. We thought we'd found it all. But your coins, and my cave, those are the first new pieces that have been discovered in a very long time."

"So you've been able to read it all translated for… how many decades?"

"Well, no. We were able to get most of the syllables teased out fairly quickly, but the true interpretation has only started in the last two decades, as we've developed sufficient basis in the sciences to understand their concepts."

"So why all the secrecy?"

"'To strive, to seek, to find, and not to yield.'"

"*Ulysses*, Lord Tennyson."

"What does that mean to you?"

"Well, Baum said it was ironic, that Ulysses was a flawed hero, rejecting social responsibility."

"Forget the modern nihilist view. I think the true meaning of that line is exactly what it says: that humanity is a being whose purpose is to grow, to discover, to improve the world around us."

"And what does that have to do with some ancient carvings, some alien script?"

"Remember how excited you were when you learned how to do something? Better, the first story you ever wrote. When you typed 'the end,' you were ecstatic, weren't you? Of course you were. We all were. But when you looked back on that story later…"

"Absolutely dreadful. A retelling of the Bible."

"Just like every other writer since the Bible was first printed. We all do that. And that's human nature. We try to learn, to discover, to create. And we're proud of our accomplishments. But when we realize just how far behind the true wave front of human knowledge we are…"

"We want to quit."

"And it's only when we don't get that crushing blow immediately that we can progress. How long had you been writing when you realized just how horrible that first story was?"

"Probably ten years."

"Exactly. You'd progressed so far beyond that Adam-and-Eve rehash that you were only embarrassed by it, but it didn't crush your dreams of being a writer, because you already were one."

"And you're saying that this language is that far beyond us?"

"Not the language, but the concepts it's communicating. You've watched the progress of science, seen how it moves. Why do we continue to research and discover?"

"Because there's so much left to learn, so many problems to solve."

"And how much research has been done in the field of library science, or the internal combustion engine?"

"Not much lately."

"Nothing at all. People look at them and think they're all tapped out, there are no great discoveries left to be made. Like the false quote attributed to Patent Office Commissioner Charles Holland Duell, who never actually said 'Everything that can be invented has been invented.' But people believe he did. So what would happen if we told the people that aliens had visited Earth 100,000 years ago, and left us plans for how to build an engine that could take us to the stars?"

"They'd be thrilled for the chance to go."

"No. Only the science fiction fans would be thrilled. The scientists working on actually getting us there would be crushed: worked their whole lives to improve propulsion science by a few percent, and along comes this ancient text that makes everything they've done, everything they could dream of their grandchildren doing, completely obsolete. And it's not just interstellar propulsion."

"So you're keeping this knowledge from the public…"

"Not *Star Trek*'s Prime Directive. That's a crock. It's not ruining a society by giving it a great leap forward. It's depressing the members of that society into not bothering to better themselves, because it's already been done."

"So you…"

"We try to nudge scientists in the right direction. Try to give out helpful hints, encourage those on the right track, hope that we can encourage people, rather than discourage them."

"And how long do you think it will take?"

"Conservative estimates say at least four hundred years. But I'm an optimist."

"Four hundred years, you're going to sit on the knowledge that we truly are not alone in the universe?"

"That's what we do. That's why I never wrote another piece of fiction after that night I sat with the previous director."

"And now you're offering me that same chance, that same opportunity for anonymity?"

"Yes and no. Late in his life, Isaac Asimov added to his three laws of robotics. Can you quote the zeroth?"

"'A robot may not harm humanity, or, by inaction, allow humanity to come to harm.'"

"Asimov understood what we're doing, without actually knowing about us. We're not robots, but we're trying to keep humanity from learning just how far behind we are, doing our best to not allow humanity to hurt itself, but instead to continue to strive, to seek...."

"So you expect me to just give up my career? Be an anonymous monk, going through the paces, knowing there's something more that man shouldn't be allowed to know?"

"It's not as bleak as all that. We're a fairly small cadre. The young man who brought you in is just a loaner: he knows nothing of what we are here, just follows orders. But you, I think, have what it takes to be involved. Remember, I did say we nudge research and 'discovery.' But we're still translating and interpreting. And those discs you brought us—"

"Brought you?"

"Semantics. While we've been talking, my staff ran a cursory inspection on them. They're almost certain the coins are data storage devices. Don't you want to help us figure out how to access that data, and interpret it?"

"Are they still out there? Will we meet them?"

"Not us. Our g-g-g-great-grandchildren? Maybe. Like I said, we're not destroying the knowledge—we're letting it out as quickly as we can without crushing the human spirit of invention. But we've also decided to modify our activities a bit. Remember all those scientists who grew up on science fiction? Well, in addition to our internal research, we've reached the point where we need to inspire the next generation of scientists into the next great leap. We need to craft hints into some things they're going to be reading. We're looking to hire a writer or two, and we think you might have what it takes."

Ego Boost
(first published in
Analog Science Fiction and Fact, March 2002)

Wilson "Bob" Tucker (1914–2006) made a habit of using his friends' names for characters in his stories. He did it so much that we now call it Tuckerizing. This story was my first time including Tuckerizations.

It grew out of one of the many, many conversations science fiction writers have with each other: why the heck do we spend so much time doing this thing which pays so little?

"You mean…?"

"Yes. We've discovered a way to tap into the human ego center. It's all very complicated, part of the time-matter-thought-energy equivalence. But suffice it to say, I started with the old saws about the power of positive thinking and it's the thought that counts, and I realized that they might literally be true."

"But then why hasn't anyone else ever discovered the ego center of the human brain?"

"Because there is no 'ego center'. It's a field generated by the entire brain. It's more akin to reading an aura. At any rate, we've discovered that people with bigger egos generate bigger ego fields, and we can tap into those fields."

"What kind of power output are you getting?"

"We'd originally hoped merely to get measurable energies. We almost gave up after the first few trials. Then I realized that perhaps grad students wouldn't be the best subjects.

"We moved on to a few open-minded faculty members, but again, with less-than-stellar results.

"Finally, I hit upon a brainstorm, and went to the drama department. Acting students led to working actors, and we eventually hauled in a few movie stars. We had some successes, and the hope of measurable energy turned into a dream of useful energy. But we realized that the average movie star craves the public adulation, which is why he needs so desperately to be in front of the people all the time. There is some ego there, but not much.

"Then we moved on to rock stars: same basic problem, though with a greater ego power output.

"Politicians… well, it was hard enough to find one willing to participate in the trial, and we kind of figured that any politician willing to test empirically the size of his ego probably didn't have a very large one. We were right."

"Then how…?"

"How are we going to the stars? Elementary. If you look at our data, you'll see there's an almost precise inverse relationship between the amount of public adulation our supposed ego hogs receive and the true strength of their egos. Politicians, movie stars, rock stars, in increasing order of strength. So we went looking for people who absolutely must have big egos to do what they do, while at the same time receiving almost no public notice."

The reporter glanced at the professor's book shelves. "You mean…?"

"Yep. Who else but the world's biggest egos could labor for months in solitude to ultimately produce something that will generate mere pennies for their time?

Science fiction authors. The starships *Ellison*, *Resnick*, and *Burstein* launch next Tuesday."

For those of you who don't recognize them: Harlan Ellison (1934–2018; wrote the Star Trek *episode "The City on the Edge of Forever" and edited the* Dangerous Visions *anthologies), Mike Resnick (1942–2020; wrote the Kirinyaga series and edited* Jim Baen's Universe *and* Galaxy's Edge *magazines), and Michael A. Burstein (1970– ; a good friend, he wrote me into a few of his stories, and edited the anthology* Jewish Futures*).*

You Gotta See This!

(first published in
Analog Science Fiction and Fact, December 2002)

At the time I wrote this, I was intensely involved with the Artemis Project, and publishing Artemis Magazine. *So why didn't I publish it in my own magazine? I didn't like the idea of vanity publishing (that's what it was called back then, before self-publishing became so respectable). Also, I have trouble with the idea of paying myself to publish my own work, but I'm quite happy to take someone else's money for my fiction.*

Besides, science fiction is a rather intimate field: when I told Stanley Schmidt I was leaving Analog *to start my own magazine, the first thing he said was "Can I send you a story?" His "Generation Gap" appeared in the first issue of* Artemis, *and was a finalist for the Hugo Award for Best Novelette.*

I guess you could call us a bunch of practical jokers. Our wives usually call us bums, our bosses call us roughnecks, and reporters—when they talk about us—spacejacks.

Building Artemis City ain't the easiest job we've ever had, but it can be interesting. And working in a low-g, no-air environment sure opened things up for some new practical jokes.

Like the time Benny smeared that real smelly cheese in Artie's air hose: Artie wasn't none too happy that night.

Or when Stu got on the radio, and made like he was from Alpha Centauri; near to scared Bobby outta his suit.

Anyway, we was all enjoying ourselves—working hard, as always—when Greg gets this idea. "Why keep joking each other? We're up here, looking down on the world," Earth is always the world, to us, "and there ain't much they can do to us. We oughta come up with the joke to end all jokes... on them."

Well, I didn't know what the joke was, but I knew it was a good idea, and I said so.

Then Joey comes along. Joey's always got the weirdest jokes. Sometimes they ain't any good, but he's more creative than the rest of us put together.

"Joey," Greg says, "what's the best way we can joke the whole world at once?"

Joey's face goes blank, so we know he's deep in thought.

"There's gonna be an eclipse of the sun Monday a week, on August 21st." We have no idea how he knows this stuff. "It'll be visible all across the States. That'd be the best time to do it, 'cause everyone will be looking up here."

"Do what?" asks Artie.

"Well, we've got all these solar furnaces, right?" The solar furnaces are big kettles with fresnel lenses on top; we use 'em to melt rocks. Anyway, Joey says, "We gotta turn the lenses over. They won't be any good for melting rocks like that, but we can put 'em back again after the joke."

"Yeah, we could do that," says Stu, "but why?"

But Joey's back to thinkin'. "And we gotta coat the insides of the furnaces with steel. Real shiny, like mirrors."

Bobby's the smelting expert. "Okay, coat the insides with high-gloss steel. Yeah, we can do that in like a day. Might not last too long, though."

"That's fine," says Joey.

Now we're gettin' into it, but he still hasn't told us what the gag is gonna be.

"A light source," he starts muttering. "We need a really bright light. Seven of them."

I figure that means one for each of us.

"The landing lights," I say. They're my department. "There won't be any ships coming in between now and the 21st, anyway, right Benny?"

Benny's the guy who keeps track of schedules. "Nope. Next one's not due in 'til the 26th."

"Okay," says Joey. "Now we're cooking. Power for the lights."

"They're plugged into the grid," says Artie, the power boss.

"Sure, they are now," says Joey. "But they're each going to need an independent power source for this to work. No way we're laying a thousand miles of power cables to pull off this gag."

"Huh?" someone asks.

"There's seven of us, which means we'll have to make due with seven points. One furnace and one light each. Each one of us is going to need a battery, Artie."

"We've still got those RTGs collecting dust. Use 'em?"

"You'll have to ramp up the power output a bit. But they ought to work."

And then we get busy. Coating the furnaces and switching the lenses are easy, but putting the lamps in and wiring them up takes a bit more work.

So anyway, we finish our super-sized flashlights, and Joey's got this map out, all marked up with tracks and seven Xs. "We need one of us at each of those spots. I've mapped out paths that the surface buggies can handle for each of us. We'll have to synchronize our watches so that we all turn them on at the same instant."

And looking closer at the map, we see the lay-out of the seven points.

"A smiley face?" I ask Joey.

"Hey, everyone's gonna be looking. And when I switch my light off and on, we'll be smiling and winking at the world."

1-9-4-Blue-3-7-2-6-
Gamma-Tetrahedron

(first published in *Nature*, January 5, 2012)

Another of my time-travel stories. And no, I've never told anyone my code.

I always knew I was destined for great things, even as a child. It was only when I started growing up that I learned how the world worked, and realized that great wealth would make those great things much easier to attain. Unfortunately, attaining great wealth wasn't quite so easy.

I didn't find my fortune on Wall Street. My writing career looked to be pleasant, but not blockbuster. Lottery wins were hard to come by. And I didn't even have a big enough stake to take the poker world by storm.

Then, one day, I hit upon the solution. It was so simple I almost laughed with joy at it.

I didn't have to find my fortune all by myself.

As long as the universe would allow time travel, my future self already knew how I'd made my fortune. With time travel, of course, he'd come back to tell me how to do it, ensuring that he would have that fortune when the time came.

So all I had to do was be prepared for my visit from my future self. Chance favors the prepared mind, and I was going to be prepared. I needed a foolproof way of recognizing my future self, because he might have only a moment to give me what I needed. He might not look like me anymore. I needed something. A recognition code. Something I would know, he would remember, and no one else would ever even think of.

1-9-4-blue-3-7-2-6-gamma-tetrahedron.

A code. A code I repeated to myself nearly constantly at first, until it became ingrained in my brain. And then only regularly, to keep it fresh, so I would recognize it instantly. Who knew? My contact with my future self might be only a few seconds. I would need to be able to hear (or see) that code and know it immediately, so as not to waste whatever brief time interval we might have together.

One-nine-four-Blue-three-seven-two-six-Gamma-Tetrahedron.

I kept plugging away, trying to write that best-selling novel (no luck yet); on Wall Street, everyone seemed to be making money but me; I hadn't yet hit a winning lottery combination. But I knew my destiny was assured. Somewhere out there was the future me who had the answers; who knew how I would make my fortune. And he'd be back to tell me. After all, he needed to tell me how to do it, so that he would have that fortune.

1-9-4-blue-3-7-2-6-gamma-tetrahedron.

I went to work for an internet start-up company, but it didn't make it out of the gate. I tried my hand at poker, but was only a fair player, and without a large enough bankroll, the big money tournaments were well out of my reach. I even started several businesses on my own and with friends, but they all came to nought.

One-nine-four-Blue-three-seven-two-six-Gamma-Tetrahedron.

There were times when I was depressed, thinking it was all a cosmic joke on me, that of course there was no way my future self would be able to tell me anything. But at my core, I held fast to that feeling; it felt so right, it made the universe make sense. It had to be. My future self would tell me how to do it.

1-9-4-blue-3-7-2-6-gamma-tetrahedron.

I tried to imagine what would be the best place, the right time for my future self to visit, to share the words or data I needed to know, and then I realized it didn't matter. My future self already knew when and where we would meet. After that meeting, I'd know it, too, and then I could remember it for us.

ONE-NINE-FOUR-BLUE-THREE-SEVEN-TWO-SIX-GAMMA-TETRAHEDRON.

It was my code. I never wrote it down; never told it to anyone; never even told anyone my code existed. It was going to work; it had to work.

1-9-4-Blue-3-7-2-6-Gamma-Tetrahedron.

One day, I was sitting in the park, reading a book, taking a break, when someone sat down on the bench beside me. "One-nine-four-blue-three-seven-two-six-gamma-tetrahedron," he said.

I dropped my book. "I've been waiting for you," I said.

"I know," he said, in a voice I'd only heard on tape. "I'm sorry to disappoint you, but we're not going to be rich anytime soon. I need a sample of your blood, to prove I've been here."

"And then what? Will we be rich after that?"

"Doubtful," the future me said. "I'm just a junior member of the team. They only chose me for the trip because I'm expendable, and because I told them I had a foolproof way of finding my earlier self. But the fabric of the universe won't allow more than three or four trips, so this is a proof-of-concept trip that will probably never be repeated."

"But what about the stock market, or the lottery, or—"

"I'm not rich in my time, so I can't help you, there. But can I have a sample of your blood?"

I sat there, stunned, while he drew a sample. Then he walked away. I didn't even pay attention.

Eight-five-omega-zero-three-three-orange. Eight-five-omega-zero-three-three-orange.

There must be an alternate universe, one in which I find my fortune, and can travel between universes to tell myself how to do it....

It's All My Fault, or,
The Beanstalk Sucks

(first published in *Nature*, May 22, 2019)

As a writer of (mostly) short-short stories, it feels like I haven't published very many words of fiction, so I tell people that I think of myself as a science fiction writer, even though the vast majority of my published words have been non-fiction (capped by The Presidential Book of Lists, Ranking the First Ladies, *and* Ranking the Vice Presidents*). It was only as I was putting this book together that I realized I have actually published a fair amount of fiction. Don't get me wrong: the published fiction words are still the minority of my professional output, but there's actually a book's worth of them? Wow!*

If I'm wrong, and somebody should actually be around to find this, I want it known that it's my fault. Not the first disaster—I didn't start the nuclear war, and I doubt anyone who's left knows who did—but the second disaster, the more catastrophic one, that's me.

I guess I was lucky to be in Quito when the world nuked itself. Apparently, the Beanstalk wasn't a target on anyone's "A" list. Either that, or whoever it *was* an A for got hit first and didn't get their turn.

Those people who talked about nuclear winter had it right—and I'm sure they'd be glad to know that. All those blasts creating all that debris, and all the fires, and atmospheric havoc, and whatnot… well, on a good day,

I can see for meters. It's all that schmutz in the air. We can't see anything, and the Sun can't warm the planet.

I know, I know. If you're human, you know all this, since you were here for it. But if I'm right, and Fermi was wrong, maybe you're not from this planet, so I'm explaining it for you.

Anyway, once before I died (and I was wondering whether it would be the radiation or freezing—who knew?), I wanted to see the Sun again. I'm not sure why, I guess it's that feeling of the "life-giving" Sun.

Like I said, Quito didn't take any direct hits, so most of the factories were still operational. Of course, the fallout from the near misses was enough to wipe out the population. Fortunately (or maybe now, unfortunately), the Beanstalk's Control Room is a concrete-and-lead bunker a klick underground. Me, Sanchez, and Johnston were on duty at the time, so we survived. There wasn't any food in the Control Room, so after a few days, I went out for a recon mission.

A flying brick had smashed the elevator's motor, as I found out when I got topside, so I had to hike up.

I couldn't find any food that had the least possibility of being safe to eat, but I figured we wouldn't last much longer anyway, and irradiated food was better than starving. While I was wandering around, seeing the remains of a recently-vibrant city, I kept looking up, searching for the Sun. I think that's when I decided I wanted to see it one more time.

Anyway, I climbed back down to tell Sanchez and Johnston that our prospects for food weren't good, but when I opened the door, I realized that neither of them wanted to live in what was left of the world… what a mess.

The diagnostics said there was an obstruction 150 klicks up, but I figured that would be high enough to get out of the gunk in the atmosphere. There was only one Cargo Lift Module available, but one was all I'd need.

I found a plastics factory, and figured out how to work the controls; thank goodness for automation. I set the machines to make a tube… a long tube… one meter in diameter, and 150 kilometers in length.

While the factory was busy extruding, I built a canister that was open on one end, which would be the bottom, and had a mirror sealed to the inside of the top. I was able to make the seal tight with rubber and sealant. A latch to open the top when it stopped moving, and I was ready to attach the plastic tube—and make the longest, and last, reflecting telescope in history.

Transporting the whole assembly to the Beanstalk was a bit of a problem, but once I got it there, hooking the canister to the CLM was a cinch.

Down to the Control Room I went, and then up the Beanstalk the canister, pulling its tube, went.

I headed for the surface, and the mirror I'd left at the base of my rising telescope. It looked like a vine growing on a tree.

I got to the base of the telescope about the same time the CLM reached the blockage up top. I saw the tube stop rising, and knew the mirror on top of the canister was opening.

There was about a klick of tube left, so I hacked through it, and tied the end down to keep it taut. Then I angled my eyepiece-mirror up the tube and looked. The Sun shined on my face, and I smiled. I felt better knowing that, even if the world was basically gone, the Sun was still there.

I felt the beginning of a breeze that quickly got stronger. It was weird—I didn't remember feeling much air movement when I was out earlier.

It kept growing, and I realized it was blowing *up* my telescope. I stared at it stupidly for a few minutes, feeling the wind grow, and then something in my head said "suction pump."

I ran down to the Control Room, but there was no way I could get the CLM to come back down—it was fouled in whatever had stopped it. Naturally, I hadn't bothered to install a closing mechanism on the canister.

I know I was going to die anyway, but there may be some people somewhere who had a chance. Who were properly shielded. What do I say now? Whoever fired the bombs probably killed off most of the human race, but there had to be some remnant left.

But now, when we run out of air…

The whistling's getting louder.

The Ant and the Grasshoppers

(first published in *Daily Science Fiction*,
November 16, 2017)

This is the first story I wrote for the anthology If We
Had Known *(see "The Necessary Enemy"), but it was
deemed too short. It was not, however, deemed
unpublishable, and the online 'zine* Daily Science Fiction
found it long enough for their audience.

The history of human achievement is the history of
saying "if only we had known." If only we had known
DDT is dangerous to mammals. If only we had known
asbestos causes lung cancer. If only we had known lead
is a neurotoxin.

But now I've been living the opposite. If only I had
never known. If only I had never known, I could have
been happy. If only I had never known that humanity
never learns, that the average human will steadfastly
refuse to be an ant, that he can only ever be the
grasshopper.

Maybe, if I could have learned to drink like my peers,
to party like my roommates… If I could have been happy
studying some meaningless liberal arts instead of the hard
sciences. If I could have convinced myself that happiness
was my right, rather than something to achieve. If I hadn't
read "Harrison Bergeron," if I hadn't striven to achieve,
I, too, could be happy. I could be out there, celebrating
with the crowd who is trying to sanctify my name.

But no. I had to be the polymath. I had to discover the
doomsday asteroid. I had to break the government gag

and announce it to the world. And then I had to be the one to invent the backstepper. And when I activate it, and the entire world jumps ten years into the past, they'll be just as happy as they were for the last ten years, knowing nothing of their impending doom. I—I alone—only I will retain the knowledge that our world is going to end in ten minutes. I'll have to live through those ten years again, to reinvent the backstepper and save all my grasshoppers again... and again... and again. If only I hadn't known, then we could all die in blissful ignorance.

But I do know. And so, once again, I will live, lonely in my foreknowledge, living in obscurity, awaiting my final moment of adulation to save them all again.

All the Things that Can't Be
(first published in
Analog Science Fiction and Fact, November 2007)

Another one of those recursive stories. And actually, most of what I've written here was true at the time: Stan's editorial, the talking fish, and the rejection letter that started it all.

Dear Stan,

I wanted to start with something cute, like "I'm sorry. Your rejection does not fit our current needs, therefore, I'll be expecting to see my story in an upcoming issue." And while that might have worked with a college admission, I've been on your side of the desk enough to know it wouldn't work here.

But then I thought a bit more about your words, when you said my story "has an interesting idea, but the overall effect is too similar to a couple of other stories I already have. Would you believe two end-of-universe stories that I *bought*, plus some others that I didn't?" After working for you for six years, and then starting my own magazine, and looking for the answer, your rejection letter may have provided the key. I think I now know what makes you such a good editor.

It isn't simply picking good stories from bad and publishing them in an interesting combination (though that's part of it). And it isn't merely helping writers who are *almost* there with their writing, to push them over the top into professional publishability (though, again, that's a part). It isn't even pushing the magazine on unsuspecting readers who desperately need to be reading it.

I think what you're doing, and what I wasn't able to do with my own magazine, is cherry-picking the brains of writers. As many times as I've asked, I can never remember which branch of physics gave you your doctorate, and I think that's by design. It isn't physics at all: it's psychics. You're using the writers who submit stories, and the stories themselves, to gain a greater insight into what's really going on in the world. At conventions, you laughingly tell tales of receiving multiple talking fish stories in one week, only to track down the strange article in some obscure newspaper that set all those writers on the same line of reasoning. And you wrote an amusing editorial about "The Ideas that Wouldn't Die," warning would-be writers to not waste their time writing the same story you've rejected hundreds of times.

But in all that time, you've also been using those statistics, the numbers of stories with the same theme, to track and tap the collective subconscious. You tracked down the source of the talking fish stories not merely for your own amusement, but to ascertain that it was a cause, and that the talking fish stories weren't prescient. And the ideas that wouldn't die are all stories that you've backtracked sufficiently that you simply *know* it isn't all a dream, or a video game, or that we're each of us Adam or Eve. So you've used Holmes' Dictum, and removed all the things that can't be.

And more than that: I've figured out why the lead time between selling you a story and seeing it in print is so long, and why you're able to live so well on an editor's salary. You're using these predictive stories to guide your own investments. Nanotechnology, biotech, virtual reality: you were in on all of them before they hit the market, because you knew they were coming through the stories you're reading and publishing. And of course, once you're properly invested, publishing the story only increases the public demand for whatever it is, driving up the value of your initial investment. You know, if you were an investment advisor, you'd be accused of artificially pumping up the prices of stocks, but as an editor, you can get away with it with impunity. I applaud your foresight (or at least, the foresight of your writers).

But now I have to ask: Have you backtracked the spate of end-of-the-universe stories you've recently seen, or should I start worrying?

Rockefeller on the Rocks
(first published in the anthology
The Fans are Buried Tales)

Several years ago, there was a science fiction convention which was extended due to a blizzard. There was no official programming on those extra days, so the stranded fans and professionals told each other stories. Taking that, and The Canterbury Tales, *as their inspiration, Peter David and Kathleen David put together the anthology* The Fans are Buried Tales, *and were gracious enough to accept a story from me. This story appears in the book as "The Conspiracy Theorist's Tale, or, Rockefeller on the Rocks."*

As I said earlier, in addition to my science fiction writing, I'm a presidential historian. I also mentioned that my presidential interests tend to the more obscure, rather than the more famous.

"You know Dick Cheney's fatal heart attack wasn't the first time they covered up a Vice President's death in office, right?"

My family and I had finished experiencing Disney World's Hall of Presidents, and had moved on to the less-well-known Broom Closet of Vice Presidents. My family's good-natured eye-rolls as I expanded upon the brief descriptions—but the stories were so fascinating!—had lost a lot of their good-naturedness, and they had abandoned me, drifting outside to wait for me to finish. But how could they not be drawn in by the story of John C. Breckinridge, the youngest vice president in American history, who—after he left office—went into exile after turning traitor (only the second vice president to do so, after Aaron Burr)? Or about how William Rufus deVane King, our first gay vice president, was the only one to be inaugurated in a foreign country? Or how Alben Barkley—for whom the term "Veep" had been coined—was the only V.P. to marry while he was serving as V.P.?

Well, apparently they'd reached their limit of being drawn into those stories, so I was looking around myself, to make sure I'd seen everything, before we headed back to the rides that drew the rest of them (the Haunted Mansion! Space Mountain! The Jungle Cruise!—yeah, sure, whatever).

This fellow popped up, looking like a cast member. But unlike all the other Disney World cast members, he seemed deadly serious, quite earnest, and not the least bit cheerful. His name tag said "James," and I remembered that was the most common first name for presidents.

"Excuse me?" I said. "Cheney's 'fatal' heart attack?"

"Sure, I thought everyone knew about that. It was in late 2007. That's why he didn't make a bid for the presidential nomination in 2008. But that's not the interesting one. You know about Nelson Rockefeller, right?"

The second Vice President to be appointed under the terms of the 25th Amendment, the most recent to be dropped from a President's re-election campaign ticket (though Gerald Ford, running with Bob Dole, lost the election to Jimmy Carter), and the only deceased President or Vice President to not be buried or otherwise entombed: Rockefeller was cremated, and his ashes spread on the family estate at Sleepy Hollow.

"Sure," I said, "I know about Nelson Rockefeller. Appointed Vice President when Ford succeeded Nixon to the Presidency, died two years after leaving office, and—"

"Not quite," said James. "He didn't make it to the end of the term. Heck, he didn't make it to the end of the year."

Rockefeller had taken office on December 19, 1974.

"Yep," he said, "and he died a week later, on Christmas. A little too much Christmas 'celebration,' if you ask me."

"What are you talking about," I said, both aggrieved and curious.

"Well… you know Rockefeller had several, uh, extramarital affairs. This one, with a young Ms. Marshack, was apparently a bit more than his aged heart could handle."

"I know that one," I said, feeling my own dander rising. "But that was in January 1979, after he'd retired from the Vice Presidency."

"Hey, the best kind of lie is one that's mostly the truth. It actually did happen, but it was on Christmas Day, 1974."

"I have to tell you, I'm having a hard time believing this. Why would 'they'—whoever 'they' are—have tried to cover it up?"

"Well…" he said conspiratorially, looking around, "after Nixon's resignation and Ford's succession, and then using the new 25th Amendment for the second time in less than two years, Rockefeller's sudden death would have meant appointing a third Vice President in the 1973–77 term, and Ford, Speaker Carl Albert, and Chief Justice Warren Burger just knew it would throw the public into further turmoil. The people needed some consistency, some calm. Especially after the resignation and the pardon. So they called in the vice president's brother, David, to act as an intermediary. David was the chairman of Chase Manhattan Bank at the time, so he came to Disney with both the family's money and the bank's to guarantee any expenses.

"You know Walt and the company are fabulously wealthy now, but at the time, they were just middlin' ultra-high wealth. The Rockefellers... well, they had lots of money. So they got together, convinced Roy and the company to build an audioanimatronic replicant of the suddenly deceased Vice President, and put the real one on ice."

Something about that paragraph stuck in my short-term memory. Actually, several things he said there. But I filed one away for later.

"So you're saying Vice President Rockefeller was a robot."

"Pretty much. That's why they kept him away from major policy decisions, away from campaigning, away from most of the things the people—and Nelson Rockefeller himself—would have expected him to do in office. He'd been governor of New York for fourteen years: he was the consummate politician, an expert in domestic policy. And when Rockefeller agreed to take the Vice Presidency, the agreement had been that he'd have a big role to play. Rockefeller the man could have done great things. But Rockefeller the animatron was... well... a little stiff."

"And who are you, to be telling me this? And why are you telling me?"

"I'll get to that. But you have to admit, several questions you had about Rockefeller make much more sense if what I'm saying is true, don't you?"

I dithered for a moment, wanting to call him out for spreading conspiracy theories, yet slotting all the pieces into place and wondering if this one actually made sense.

"That's one of the reasons Vice President Rockefeller never moved into the Vice President's Residence at the Naval Observatory: having to recharge the Vice President every night would surely have drawn a little too much attention from people whose silence couldn't be guaranteed."

Now he was going too far, but dammit, he'd drawn me in. "You said Walt and the company *are* fabulously wealthy. But didn't he die in in 1966?"

"Well, 'died' is a term that has shades. He was declared dead, but I'm sure you've heard the rumor that he was cryogenically preserved. Actually, he was in the next tank over from Vice President Rockefeller."

Before I could say anything to that, there was some rustling behind a utilidoor, and another cast member stepped out, saying "James, could you come with me for a moment?" The hand he put on James' arm seemed anything but polite.

"I'll be right back," James said to me with a catch in his throat, and they both disappeared through the utilidoor.

I heard the sounds of a tussle, some low-pitched voices, and it was more than just a moment. I waited.

It was probably ten minutes later when James came back, though his eyes seemed a bit glassy, his expression somewhat rigid.

"Everything okay?" I asked.

"Of course," he said, sounding a little less animated. "The Disney experience is all about bringing you in to this fantasy world, so like—and yet so unlike—the real world outside. I just knew you'd be drawn in by the story."

"So now you're saying it's just a story? There was no animatronic Nelson Rockefeller?"

"Of course not. Don't you think someone would have noticed?"

"And Walt Disney isn't really cryogenically frozen back there somewhere?"

"Oh, sure he is. And I'm just a robot, too." His eyelid shivered into an approximation of a wink.

Then he turned, opened the utilidoor… and I saw oil dripping from the cuff of his pants.

Grignr in the Land of Er-Urz

(first appeared in the anthology
*The Eye of Argon and the Further Adventures of
Grignr the Barbarian*)

*"The Eye of Argon" is a classic piece of bad fantasy
fiction—known more for its typos and word infelicities
than for its story—about which an entire mythos has
grown, to the point that I'm part of a troupe who perform
the story at science fiction conventions. After several years
of doing the same performance, we decided to expand our
repertoire and also extend the lore surrounding "The Eye
of Argon" and its hero, Grignr, by writing sequels and
publishing an anthology. But we wanted to be true to the
original: typos, poor word choices, and all.*

*Just remember, this story is supposed to be bad. Oh,
and as for the chapter numbers: that's another homage
to the original (yes, there really is a chapter 3 ½ in the
original story).*

– 1 –

The muscle-bound Ecordian came across a cadre of
prostitutes who had spent the night singing lustfully, and
as a consequence, the whores were hoarse. But they
would not due to carry Grignr onward. Neither wood the
ability to construct him a vessel to sale the reever through
these lands.

"What you need," cried the narrator, "is a mighty
weapon!"

"Quill I find it nearby?" beseeched the breach-clouted
clod.

"Mightier than that petty blade you carry, seek in the animal enclosure. There you will find the pen, which is indeed mightier than the flown bird."

"Flown bird? Soared?"

"Aye, there's the cub. This device, called 'editor,' can set you to rites."

"Gods have nought to do—"

"Take it, take it!" screamed the long-suffering audience.

Shruffing his showeders, Grignr took the pen of correction, and felt grate power coarsing threw hymn.

"With this, I will be the master of all I sorbet. I will reed and rite, and possibly even rithmetic, as we travail two the three-lined hell sides of yon mondegreen verdant… Wait!" yelled he who was strong like a bull and smart like a tractor—"even eye ken sea this cursed tulle is knot—"

The narrator's laughter cut Grignr off mid-malapropism.

"Your pardon, grated one," wheezed the narrator. "You have taken up the typo maker, not the typo braker. But as shadows are not seen without light, nor good recognized in the absence of evil, the fixer can only be found with the maker. As thou travelest the Fleetest of Streets, passed the Grayest of Ladies, toward the Stiles of Manualism, seek that which seekst that which you carry, and all shall be as blew penciled."

Muddering under his braeth at the horrer thus inflicted upon himself—knot to menshun his long-suffering readers—Grignr took the maker of typographic Er-urz, smote the narrator, and took his leave of the hoarse horseless whores.

This, thought Grignr, is what I get for destroying the idle in Chapter 6 of the original story.

As the sun descended into the crimson west, the gathering darkness made it too difficult for the narrator to follow the action....

– 1 ½ –

It was night, too dark to see the page clearly enough to continue writing the story. And so, the narrator did not.

– 2 –

After the long night of terrible travails—thankfully illegible to the poor readers do to the dark—a new day dawned, giving the narrator leave to continue telling the tall tail.

As Grignr reached the trees, he considered the wood about him. Riding all through the night and the rising dawn on the sway-backed horse he had acquired through the incredible deeds of derring-did which remain invisible in Chapter 1 ½, Grignr ached of the road. Perhaps, thought he, I can use some of this lumbar for a little lumber support.

If only he cud klew in on his indeterminate destination, the location of the typo braker, to cleanse his pallet and the readers's reeding materiel.

Unfortunately, an easy solution did not present itself, and the narrator knew Grignr was to remain part of the precipitant. Grignr, of course, did not understand the pun, nor did he understand the concept of a precipitants and solutions.

At any rate, Grignr continued his journey, occasionally looking at the typo maker the narrator had gifted him in Chapter 1. The maker, for its part, quivered eagerly in the direction of its counterpart, leading Grignr ever onward, ever upward, ever ward.

– 3 –

Thus it was, after many long traverses, that Gringr found his way to the editorial office of the great and mighty publisher, the one—blessed be he—who might indeed no the weigh to correct the text, and save the readers.

"Stand, dog," snarled the savage Accordion. "Long have I traveled, far have I ventured, that I mite at this anointed our make good on the please of our reeders, to be able to find there weigh threw the horrid spelling of which I, personally, no knot.

"Wherefore, there [the narrator interjects to note that the proper phrasing should, 'Therefore, where…', though he fears it's a losing cause to seek proper spelling or phrasing at this point] have you hidden this marvelous tool, this maker of cents?"

Standing, the editor reached into his pocket protector—fairly bursting with pens, pencils, and other such writing implements—and pulled forth a magically glowing blue pencil.

"This, noble knight, this is that which you seek. The blue pencil of correction, long eschewed by the larger publishers seeking to save a buck. With it, your horrible misspellings and awkward utterances will be a thing of the past. Clarity will reign, and your readers shall know the joy of enjoying your story."

"Give it to me!" screamed Grignr! "Let me dew what I may."

"There is but one problem, Grinder," said the editor. "One that I fear will continue to plague us for an endless time."

Gringr felt the swaet braeming on his brow.

"In this land, no one has yet invented the pencil sharpener."

Grignr unleashed his sword, slew the editor, and declared the absurdity at...

An End.

Get me to the job on time
(first appeared in
Analog Science Fiction and Fact, May 2003)

I'm a good worker: I get my work done on time, even if I have to stay late. But I'm not a morning person. My biggest problem, when I was working in the corporate world, was being at my desk at 9:00 AM. In my opinion, mornings would be great if they started about noon.

The idea for this story came to my while I was standing on the platform, waiting for my train to work, and running late, again.

"Maybe it's what you'd do with the knowledge that determines whether or not you'll discover the secret of time travel."

"What?" I asked the old man.

"I know for a fact that time travel is possible. I knew the man who discovered it. And you'll never guess what he used his discovery for."

Well, I didn't believe that old man any more than you believe me, but we'd been waiting in that airport for four hours, so I humored him.

"All right, I'll bite," I said. "What did he use time travel for?"

"Wally didn't need to see the pyramids getting built, or sail with Columbus, or even watch JFK's assassination. What Wally wanted to do, more than anything, was get to work on time."

An introduction like that demands a story, so I sat down and let him tell me.

* * *

Wally didn't want fame [the old man said]. I think he would have been perfectly happy if no one but the payroll department knew his name. Did I mention we both worked in the same department?

Anyway, he loved his job. We were editors, and Wally simply loved being an editor; always got his work done on schedule, never made any mistakes, and there was no place he'd rather be.

But he had one big problem at work: Wally just could not get to work by 9 A.M.

Some days it was a common excuse—train delays, doctor appointments, plumbing emergencies. And sometimes, the damnedest things happened to him—he got caught in hold-ups, subway hijackings, rat stampedes. Anything and everything, it seemed, conspired to keep Wally from getting to work on time.

And he could never understand it. On the one hand, his work was always done on time, and his lateness never affected anyone else—if I wanted to talk to Wally, I knew I had to wait 'til late morning. On the other hand, he tried his hardest to get in on time, and the few times he made it, he'd usually left the house three hours early, and had been at his desk since 6:30. He just couldn't win.

I never believed in a determinist universe, but in Wally's case, I was starting to make an exception.

Discovering time travel, I think, was his calling. If he hadn't, the perversity of the universe would have been proven beyond all doubt.

One Monday, Wally and I both walked in the door at 9 on the dot. He wasn't a few minutes late, nor screamingly early; he was precisely on time.

"Wally!" I said, "I'm stunned!"

"That's two of us," he said, and sat down to get to work.

I let the incident go, chalking it up to blind chance. I mean, if you're working in a place for a couple of years, the odds have to favor walking in the door at 9 A.M. at least once, right?

Well, the next morning, wouldn't you know it, he and I were in the same elevator, and on our floor at 9 on the tick.

"Okay, Wally," I said. "Two days in a row you're on time. What gives? Are you leaving three hours early, and then waiting for me to get here on time?"

"No, no," he stammered. "Nothing like that. It's just… well… I think I've finally figured out how to get here on time."

"How'd you do it?" I asked.

"Can you keep a secret?" I nodded. "I've discovered the secret of time travel."

And he clammed up. Wouldn't say another word. I looked over at him every now and again throughout the day, and when he caught my eye, he'd wink and smile a little, so I wasn't sure if he'd been pulling my leg or not.

Come Friday, I couldn't stand it. I sidled up to Wally's desk about 9:30, and whispered to him, "Time travel, huh?"

"Mmm hmm," he said.

"So what time did you leave home to get here at 9?"

"You won't believe me," he said.

"Try me."

"Today, I woke up at noon, watched the news, showered, ate breakfast about one this afternoon, took an uncrowded subway ride in to work, got to the lobby about quarter to two this afternoon, and then time-traveled back to 8:57 this morning. Then I stepped out from behind that big potted fern and joined the throng jostling for the elevators."

"Do you really expect me to believe that cockamamie story?" I asked him.

"No, not really. But it's the truth." And he went back to work.

I sat down at my desk, staring at the papers in front of me and not seeing them. Then I gave up. I dialed Wally's home phone number. It rang five times, and I was looking at Wally the whole time. On the sixth ring, a groggy Wally picked up; I knew his voice. I'm listening to Wally wake up on the phone while I'm watching him working at his desk not ten feet from me.

I hung up and went back to Wally's desk.

"Oh, yeah," he said, "Before I woke up at noon, the phone woke me sometime in the morning, but there was no one there."

I left the company a few years later, but by that time, I believed him. I think he really had found the secret to time travel.

I asked him about it at my going-away party. "If you've really discovered time travel, what are you going to do with it?"

"What do you mean, 'do with it'?" he asked. "I get to work on time. Isn't that enough?"

And the thing about Wally was, getting to work on time really was enough for him.

Then our flight was called. I boarded early to get to my seat in the back, while the old man waited for his row to be called. I figured I wouldn't see him again.

On the plane, however, he smiled at me as I walked to the back.

And we landed two hours early.

"Mars is the Wrong Color" first published in *Nature*, 2 October 2008.

"It's the Thought That Counts" first published in *Analog Science Fiction and Fact,* April 1998.

"The Necessary Enemy" first published in *If We Had Known*, edited by Mike McPhail, eSpec Books, May 2017.

"Creatively Ignorant" first published in *Footprints in the Stars*, edited by Mike McPhail, eSpec Books, July 2019.

"Ego Boost" first published in *Analog Science Fiction and Fact*, March 2002.

"You Gotta See This!" first published in *Analog Science Fiction and Fact*, December 2002.

"1-9-4-blue-3-7-2-6-gamma-tetrahedron"   first published in *Nature*, 5 January 2012.

"It's All My Fault, or, The Beanstalk Sucks" first published in *Nature*, 22 May 2019.

"The Ant and the Grasshoppers" first published in *Daily Science Fiction*, 16 November 2017.

"All the Things That Can't Be" first published in *Analog Science Fiction and Fact*, November 2007.

"The Conspiracy Theorist's Tale (or, Rockefeller on the Rocks)" first published in *The Fans are Buried Tales*, edited by Peter David & Kathleen David, Crazy 8 Press, May 2022.

"Grignr in the Land of Er-Urz" first published in *The Eye of Argon and the Further Adventures of Grignr the Barbarian*, edited by Michael A. Ventrella, Fantastic Books, November 2022.

"Get Me to the Job on Time" first published in *Analog Science Fiction and Fact*, May 2003.

About the Author

Ian Randal Strock says he plays with words for money: he writes speculative fiction (having read this book, you've probably figured that out), but he writes even more non-fiction (capped by three books: *The Presidential Book of Lists* [Random House, 2008], *Ranking the First Ladies* [Carrel Books, 2016], and *Ranking the Vice Presidents* [Carrel Books, 2016]). He was first paid for his writing while he was a high school student: he sold a puzzle to *Games Magazine*. His first professional fiction sale appeared in the September 1992 issue of *Analog Science Fiction and Fact*.

However, he learned quite early that the best way to ruin a writing career is to work as an editor: he's been on the editorial staffs of *Analog*, *Asimov's Science Fiction*, Baen Books, *The Daily Free Press* (Boston), *KISS: The Official Magazine*, *Realms of Fantasy*, *Science Fiction Chronicle*, and many more. He edited and published *Artemis Magazine* and SFScope.com, and is now the owner and editor-in-chief of Gray Rabbit Publications/ Fantastic Books (www.FantasticBooks.biz).

Outside of word-work, he has worked on Wall Street, as a teacher, for an internet start-up, with a commercial aerospace start-up, and as a tour guide at Niagara Falls. He has held a slew of elected volunteer positions, and is currently the First Vice Chair of American Mensa. Ian's name is unique on the web, and his electronic home is www.IanRandalStrock.com.

Printed in the USA
CPSIA information can be obtained
at www.ICGtesting.com
JSHW022103110824
67846JS00002B/10